SATAN LIVES

A stooped figure emerged through the doorway and stood upright in the dust.

Kirk stared. His jaw went slack from astonishment. This must be a Danon, he realized.

The creature was naked—a male—and barely a meter tall. Its smooth skin was a gentle copper color. The head contained two narrow black eyes, a pair of broad flat nostrils, and a thin lipless mouth. The skull, like the body, was hairless. A pair of slightly curved horns perhaps three inches long protruded from the back of the head. The creature had a tail. It reached nearly to the ground and had a barbed tip at the end.

Kirk couldn't control his wonder.

The creature was an exact replica of Earth's most dreaded legendary being.

The Danon was a devil.

Don't miss any of these exciting classic *Star Trek* titles from Bantam Books!

DEVIL WORLD

Gordon Eklund

BANTAM BOOKS
NEW YORK • TORONTO • LONDON • SYDNEY • AUCKLAND

DEVIL WORLD

A Bantam Spectra Book

PUBLISHING HISTORY

Bantam edition / November 1979
Bantam reissue edition / November 1995

ISBN 0-553-24677-1

Published simultaneously in the United States and Canada

Bantam Books are published by Bantam Books, a division of Bantam Doubleday Dell Publishing Group, Inc. Its trademark, consisting of the words "Bantam Books" and the portrayal of a rooster, is Registered in U.S. Patent and Trademark Office and in other countries. Marca Registrada. Bantam Books, 1540 Broadway, New York, New York 10036.

PRINTED IN THE UNITED STATES OF AMERICA

RAD   0 9 8 7 6 5 4 3

PROLOGUE

Six neatly uniformed men materialized in the center of the forest clearing and glanced anxiously around for indications of life.

In the official records of the United Federation of Planets, this world was coded NC513-II; more familiarly, it was known as Heartland. An M-type planet, perfectly suited for human habitation, rich in all necessary resources, Heartland had only recently been colonized by a group of one hundred men and women, most drawn from Earth's teeming numbers. Now an anonymous distress signal emanating from Heartland had been received at Starbase 13. A ship had been sent in response to that call. These six men were from that ship.

As the men watched, the colonists emerged from the surrounding forest. The commander of the mission, Lieutenant Radly Marcus, was puzzled. Why were the colonists all gathered here at this one spot? Why weren't they waiting at their own homes sprinkled throughout the forest and nearby meadows?

Marcus decided he had better find out.

He was thirty-three years old. A hard-nosed, keen-eyed veteran of Star Fleet, Marcus liked to boast that he had seen everything the universe had to offer at least once and often as many as four and five times.

As soon as he had stepped forward and examined the colonists, Marcus had to admit that he'd told a lie.

He had never seen anything like this in his life.

The colonists numbered close to one hundred. Men and women appeared in nearly equal proportions. Their ages ranged from the low teens to the high forties.

Every last one of them—male and female, old and young—was stark, raving mad.

They babbled. They screamed. They howled and wailed. Many wept. They tore at their clothes, rolled on the ground, swung sticks and clubs at their own faces. A few, catatonic, did not move at all.

Using his portable communicator, Marcus called the mother ship, explained the situation, and recommended immediate evacuation. A medical team arrived soon after and prepared the colonists for transport. Marcus tried to question a few, but the answers he received failed to make sense.

Then he thought about the native aliens. Wasn't it likely that these creatures might have some inkling of what had occurred among the colonists? Marcus knew that the aliens lived in a nearby village. He took his five crewmen and set off through the forest.

The native inhabitants of Heartland were known as Danons. A humanoid species, they were an ancient race, having once established a civilization that at its peak had spanned half the Galaxy.

Marcus reached the village and found several hundred mud-and-grass huts. This was all that remained of the once mighty Danon civilization.

He entered the village. It seemed deserted. Not a soul stirred.

In a clearing at the center of the village, a stone tower rose twenty meters into the sky. The structure was formed in the shape of the letter Y, with an additional horizontal bar placed across the top. The base of the tower was not solid. There was a doorway. Marcus peered inside, but the hollow room within was empty.

His men gasped.

Marcus turned.

They were no longer alone. In sinister silence the aliens had arrived and now stood two deep in a circle around the clearing.

When he saw the Danons, Marcus also gasped. He felt cool shivers racing across his skin. The hair on the back of his neck seemed to stand on end.

Once again Marcus knew himself to be a liar. He had never seen anything in his life like this either.

1

With the *Enterprise* now undergoing general maintenance here at Starbase 13, I've decided to take advantage of the opportunity by issuing an order for full shore leave commencing at once and continuing until further notice. After the lengthy duration of our last voyage, the crew has shown no hesitancy in taking complete advantage of the superb facilities available here for rest, recreation, pleasure, and delight.

Holding his hands high over his head, the magician brought his heels together and executed a stiff bow as the audience that filled most of the tables below the stage rewarded him with a sustained burst of enthusiastic applause. Beside the magician on a wooden table lay the supine form of a very pretty young lady, neatly severed at the waist.

"I've heard about sawing girls in half all my life," said Dr. Leonard McCoy, chief medical officer of the starship *Enterprise*, as he clapped his hands with the others, "but I never thought I'd actually see it done."

"It is impressive," Captain James Kirk said. "Of course, it'll be even more impressive if the magician manages to put the pieces back together."

Kirk and McCoy sat with Mr. Spock, the *Enterprise's* Vulcan first officer, at a table near the front of the club room.

"A rather elementary illusion, actually," Mr. Spock said drily, as the applause slowly subsided. Spock's expression showed a slight frown, more of concentration than displeasure.

"You think you know how he does it?" McCoy said, reaching for his drink—Kentucky bourbon, unprocessed, or so the waiter claimed. "If you do, how about letting us in on the secret?"

Spock peered at the stage. "It's a matter of mirrors. Three of them, I would suspect. One on each side of the stage and a third at the rear."

"Mirrors?" said McCoy, wrinkling his brow. "I don't see any mirrors. All I see is the magician and the girl."

"The point of such mirrors," Spock said, "is that one cannot see them. Surely, Dr. McCoy, you are not offering a magical explanation."

"Oh, no. It's a trick and I know it's a trick but, damn it, Spock, the fun in a show like this comes from the illusion of reality, the suspension of disbelief. That girl looks to me like she's been cut in half. I know she hasn't been, but I prefer to pretend that she has."

"I find no pleasure in being deceived."

"It's not deception. It's a game. We—"

"Gentlemen," Captain Kirk said. "Can't we concentrate on the entertainment on the stage?" Kirk was grinning. This quarrel between Spock and McCoy was only part of a long-standing debate between them concerning the subject of reason versus emotion. "Let's watch the show."

The three of them focused their attention on the stage. The magician—who billed himself as Dr. Faustus—was dressed in a devil suit, complete with horns and tail. A thin black mustache tucked under his nose added to his Satanic facade.

Stepping to the front of the stage, the magician addressed his audience in a thin reedy voice. "Ladies and gentlemen, may I have your attention, please? Because of the acclaim you have awarded me, I find myself nearly at a loss for words. So much at a loss for words, in fact—this is terribly embarrassing—that I fear I may have forgotten the exact incantation now necessary to make my pretty young friend whole again."

A murmur of delighted laughter floated through the room, but there was a slightly nervous tinge to it. Even Kirk couldn't help wondering: what if this wasn't a joke? What if the magician really was telling the truth?

"I must ask for your indulgence," the magician said. "May I have silence? Complete and absolute silence?"

Amazingly, as the magician turned to the table where the severed girl lay, he got exactly what he had asked for. The room fell silent. Even the waiters froze in their tracks. Not a glass tinkled.

The magician threw back his head, shut his eyes, and rocked on his heels. "*Avoo,*" he said softly, barely a whisper. "*Avoo-abboo-akkuu.*" His hands passed through the air above the girl's body. "*Avoo-abboo-akkuu.*" He spoke more firmly, louder. "*Avoo-abboo-akkuu.*" Leaning down, he opened his eyes and stared straight at the girl's face. Then he drew back. "*Avoo-abboo-akkuu.* You are whole again. You are fine."

If anything, the silence thickened. No one even seemed to be breathing.

The girl stood up. It took Kirk a long moment to comprehend what this meant: if the girl could stand and move, she must be whole again.

The magician took the girl by the hand and led her around the table. The audience erupted at last in frenzied applause.

"Well," said McCoy, through the clamor, "now what do you think, Mr. Spock?"

"Since the woman was never in any legitimate danger," Spock said, "no miracle was necessary to save her."

"Only another trick?"

"Not even that."

Before the argument could gather momentum, a waiter appeared magically at Kirk's elbow. As a captain, he seldom had to wait long to be served. After McCoy had requested another bourbon, Kirk decided to have a drink of his own. "A spacerigger's delight," he said, with as much aplomb as he could manage.

McCoy made an anguished sound in his throat. "You'll kill yourself with that stuff, Jim."

"But it's a spaceman's drink, Bones. I am a spaceman."

"It's a spacerigger's drink, whatever the hell they are. Look, if you want my opinion—my medical opinion—you'll call back that waiter and plead temporary insanity."

"Nonsense," said Kirk, slapping his stomach. "The trouble with you, Bones, is you've never learned how to enjoy yourself."

McCoy made a disgusted face, and Kirk laughed. He couldn't be sure whether he'd ordered the drink for his own pleasure or merely to irritate poor McCoy.

The magician was addressing his audience again. "Ladies and gentlemen, I now intend to offer as a grand finale to the evening's entertainment a very special presentation. As you may have noted from the trim of my costume, I am not wholly unacquainted with a certain denizen of Earth's nether regions: namely, the devil. In his honor—and yours as well—I now present a feat unparalleled in the history of magic. Ladies and gentlemen, I now give you—direct from hell—through the courtesy of Satan himself—two dozen living, breathing demons."

But Kirk was no longer listening to the magician. A woman had entered the room and Kirk, along with everyone else, was watching her, transfixed. The woman was about thirty years of age, tall, white-skinned, with a lustrous crown of black hair piled on top of her head. She wore a thin ankle-length gown that flowed with her long graceful strides. Pretty was too inconsequential a term to describe the woman. She was strikingly beautiful, despite the fact that a goodly portion of her face could not be seen. A white surgical mask concealed her lips, nose, and chin from view.

Even the magician paused for a moment, staring at the woman, before turning and moving to the rear of the stage.

The woman found a vacant table close to Kirk and sat down. Above the mask, her eyes were riveted upon the stage.

2

"Remarkable," Dr. Leonard McCoy said softly.

Spock turned and looked at him in surprise. "What, Doctor? The magician?"

"I mean that woman," said McCoy. "Don't tell me you didn't notice."

"The one who entered just now? A lovely woman, I admit, but is that necessarily remarkable?"

"Even when she's wearing a surgical mask? A surgical mask here where the air's as pure as any in the universe?"

"Perhaps she has a medical reason," Kirk suggested, drawing his eyes away from the woman at last.

"She may be a Jain," Spock suggested. "At least that was my first impression."

"A Jain?" said McCoy. "What's that?"

"An ancient Earth religious faith, an offshoot of traditional Hinduism. Jainism was founded by the sage Mahavira in the sixth century before Christ."

"But why the oxygen mask?"

"To avoid accidentally harming or killing any form of life," Spock said. "Jains are noted for their reverence for life. They divide conscious matter into five general classifications, or *kivas*, according to the number of senses each entity possesses. The first classification, for instance, includes all those things possessing only touch: clay, chalk, rain, dew, fog—"

"Fog?" said McCoy, apparently bewildered by Spock's ready flow of data. "I thought we were talking about living things."

"To a Jain even the fog is alive. It possesses a soul, the same as you or I. In fact, since Jains believe in reincarnation, your soul or mine may eventually end up there."

"Yours, I hope," said McCoy.

Spock stared at him. "I believe the nature of one's next life depends upon how well one has lived this life, Doctor."

The magician appeared ready to go on with his show. He stood in the center of the stage and waved his arms over his head in opposite circles. His lips were moving, chanting, but his actual words were not loud enough to decipher. As he moved, churning his arms, a thin mist began to spread across the floor of the stage. As Kirk watched, thoroughly transfixed, the mist thickened, obscuring the figure of the magician himself.

Then the demon appeared. At first it was merely a dark shape within the mist, but gradually the shape assumed a definite form. It had arms—four of them —and legs—just two—and a huge misshapen head. The mist parted and Kirk could see the face.

He felt ill. Even during his worst nightmares, he had never conceived of anything this hideous. The demon squatted naked on its haunches, mouth open, spittle dripping. Its green skin was covered with hundreds of tiny red warts. A pair of curved tusks extended from the lower jaw, and its eyes were like two bloody sores.

The magician continued to chant. His voice was louder now, but the language was unfamiliar to Kirk.

A second demon was now materializing beside the first. This one proved to be even more grotesque than the other, with two heads instead of one and three sharp horns sprouting from the top of both skulls.

A third demon was appearing.

"If I throw up," McCoy said, "allow me to apologize in advance."

"Mere illusion," Spock said stiffly. "The magician has an excellent imagination—that's all."

Kirk found solace in Spock's rational thinking. "Of course it's a trick," he said.

"Yeah," McCoy agreed, "but how would you like to have an imagination like that?"

The third demon was a female, with three eyes, breasts like inflated bladders, and feet the size and shape of shovels.

A fourth demon was appearing.

A fifth.

A powerful odor enveloped the room. Kirk felt even sicker than before. It was the scent of decay, of putrescence and death. All right, he felt like shouting at the magician. You've given us a show. Now let up. Now quit.

Someone screamed.

The sound, shrill and horrified, snapped the magician's spell. Kirk turned and saw the woman with the surgical mask standing beside her table, a finger pointed at the stage. "You!" she cried. "You took him!" Her finger was aimed not at the magician but at the demons. "You took my father!"

Lunging forward, she rushed the stage. As she passed, Kirk reached out and caught her arm. "Wait," he said. "It's only a trick. You shouldn't let—"

Above her mask the woman's eyes bulged crazily. She gave a muffled cry and tried to break free of Kirk's grasp. Suddenly, her feet slipped from under her. She started to fall. Kirk caught her body in his arms before she struck the floor. Out of the corner of an eye he noticed to his astonishment that the stage was bare. The magician, the demons, the mist—all had vanished.

Dr. McCoy hurried around the table, reaching for the medikit he wore on his belt. The woman was unconscious. "Put her on the floor," McCoy said. "I imagine it's shock but I'd better be sure."

Kirk laid the woman gently on the carpeted floor. McCoy knelt beside her, feeling for a pulse. After a moment's hesitation, he reached up and removed her surgical mask.

Kirk gazed at the woman's face. As he had expected, she was beautiful, her features as delicate and finely drawn as classic sculpture.

McCoy looked up, a worried expression on his face. "I think this may be serious. We'd better find a place where I can examine her thoroughly."

3

The manager of the club appeared, an expression of worried concern on his round plump face, and offered Dr. McCoy the use of his private office, a cluttered cubicle to the left of the stage. Kirk carried the woman into the room and placed her on a portable cot. He stepped back, while McCoy crouched down beside her. "I think she may be suffering from acute malnutrition," he said, after a brief examination. "I'd need better facilities to make a definite diagnosis, but that could well have contributed to her faintness."

"She'll be all right?" Kirk said.

"Oh, sure. If I wanted, I could wake her right now."

"Then you don't think it was just that show."

"I'm sure it didn't help." McCoy was reading the woman's blood pressure, using a glass instrument the size and shape of a compass. "Fun is fun, but that gaggle of demons was simply grotesque. That wasn't magic. It was a freak show."

"But impressive," Spock said, from close to the doorway.

"It was that." McCoy leaned back. "I think I'll

14

try a vitamin injection." He removed an air-powered hypodermic from his medikit and injected a clear fluid through the cloth of the woman's sleeve.

The vitamin had an immediate effect. The woman opened her eyes. She looked at McCoy, then at Kirk, and put her hands to her mouth. "My mask. What have you done with it?"

"It's here," McCoy said. He picked the mask off the floor where he had let it drop and handed it to the woman. She made no attempt to put it back on.

"Who are all of you?" she asked.

"My name is Leonard McCoy. I'm a doctor. This is Captain Kirk of the starship *Enterprise* and Mr. Spock, first officer aboard the same ship."

The woman shut her eyes and made as if to sit up. McCoy pushed her gently down. "Not too quickly," he said.

She opened her eyes. "Then please tell me where I am. What happened to me?"

"You fainted, I'm afraid. Do you remember anything? The magician was putting on a show. You stood up and screamed and—"

"I remember," she said quickly. She looked at the surgical mask in her hands. "I suppose I don't really need to wear this here."

"I wouldn't think so. The air here is completely purified."

"Then I won't bother."

"May I ask you something?" McCoy said.

"Yes. You helped me."

"I'd like to know the substance of your normal diet. What foods do you usually eat and how much?"

"You think I'm suffering from malnutrition."

He nodded. "It's one possible explanation for why you fainted."

"Well, you're right. I do have malnutrition."

"Well, if there's anything we can do, anything you need to help . . ." He broke off, embarrassed.

She seemed puzzled for a long moment, then suddenly laughed, a vibrant throaty sound. "Oh, it's not money," she said. "I'm a Jain. Do you know what that is, Doctor?"

McCoy looked at Spock and nodded. "'It's an offshoot of the traditional Hindu faith founded in the sixth century B.C. by the sage—"

"Then you must understand the reasons for my diet."

"Well, as a matter of fact . . ." It was plain from McCoy's expression that he did not understand. Turning, he looked to Spock for help.

"The Jains," said Spock, "are strict vegetarians. The more devout, in fact, prefer to limit their dietary intake to such foods as berries, nuts, leaves, roots, and simple grains."

"I try to eat nothing more complex than rice," the woman said. "Away from Earth that can be a difficult regimen to maintain."

"Do you use vitamin supplements?" McCoy said.

"Never. They aren't strictly forbidden, I suppose, but I happen to believe chemistry cannot provide a road to salvation. Don't you agree, Doctor?"

McCoy spread his hands. "Then there doesn't appear to be a great deal I can do to help you. I want to warn you, though, that if you keep going the way you are, you're apt to end up in an early grave."

"If you were as familiar with my religion as you claim, you'd realize what an empty threat that is."

"Remember, the Jains believe in reincarnation," Spock said.

"Oh," said McCoy.

"So you see," the woman said, "when I die is of no particular concern to me. It's the nature of my next life that matters."

"I suppose that's your right to believe."

"Thank you, Doctor. Now may I sit up?"

"If you feel strong enough."

The woman came to her feet in a swift, graceful motion. "I do." She looked at each of them in turn. "I owe you an apology. I haven't even introduced myself. My name is Gilla Dupree."

"Not the Gilla Dupree," Kirk said, automatically.

She laughed. "As far as I know, I'm the only one."

"The senso-artist? The composer of—?"

"*Birth of a Living Star?* Yes, that one, and the others, too." Plainly, Gilla Dupree was well accustomed to her status as a celebrity.

"It's a privilege to meet you," Kirk said. "I'm a great admirer of your work." Gilla Dupree was undoubtedly the most talented senso-artist who had ever lived. Senso-drama, a synthesis of symphonic music and holographic storytelling, was a relatively youthful art form but one that Gilla Dupree had very much mastered. Kirk recalled the first time he had played *Birth of a Living Star* and how it had taken him an additional five hours to recover sufficiently from the three-hour performance to feel strong enough to leave his chair.

"I am also a great admirer," Mr. Spock said. "After Shakespeare and Tolstoy, I regard your work as the Earth's most sustained achievement in the dramatic arts."

"That's a considerable compliment," Gilla said, "coming from a Vulcan."

"And coming from a human," Spock said, "your work is awesome."

Kirk had not been aware of Spock's interest in senso-drama. He found it a bit difficult to comprehend. How could someone who claimed to be without emotion find merit in such a totally emotional form?

"Now if you gentlemen don't object," she said briskly, "I really ought to be going. There's someone I came to see."

Kirk blocked her exit. He wasn't exactly sure why. He knew only that he wasn't ready to let her leave yet. "The magic show is over, I'm afraid. The audience has undoubtedly left."

"Oh, damn." She bit her lip. "He promised to meet me after the show."

"Well, it wasn't your fault. Those demons—or whatever they were—would upset anyone."

"I guess I'm more superstitious than I like to think."

"You accused them of taking your father. Do you remember saying that? What did you mean?"

Her frown seemed genuine enough. "I don't know. My father is the reason I'm here, you see. Years ago we were separated. I've spent a great deal of time and money trying to locate him. The man I was supposed to see after the show supposedly knows something. Perhaps I just had him on my mind."

"Undoubtedly," said Kirk. Gilla no longer showed any strong inclination to leave. He knew he was deliberately prolonging their conversation. "Perhaps you should tell us more about it. We might be able to help."

"You?" She seemed surprised. "Why should you?"

"If your father's somewhere out here in space, we might have met him ourselves."

"I don't think so." She acted inwardly amused. "That large ship that just docked—is that yours?"

Kirk nodded. "The *Enterprise*."

"Then maybe you can help me. Not now, but later, after I've found out exactly where my father is. I'll need some way to get there from here."

The *Enterprise* was hardly designed for use as an interstellar ferry, but Kirk did not wish to discourage Gilla from further contact. "Perhaps we could help.

When you know something definite, why don't you come and see me?"

"I'll be sure to do that, Captain Kirk." Her smile was radiant.

After she had gone, Mr. Spock was the only one of them to find the right words to express the feeling they shared: "A most remarkable woman," he said simply.

4

As Kirk slid into the soft chair opposite the huge desk of Commodore Wilhelm Schang, he said admiringly, "This is quite a place you have here, sir." The walls of the vast office were lined with dozens of tridee prints, several of which were presently in motion. "Compared to what we were used to, it's as plush as a palace."

Commodore Schang frowned. He was a big man, with broad shoulders, a strong face, and short metal-gray hair. As a young lieutenant, Kirk had served under Schang aboard the old *Tresher*. "Too damned plush for a man like me," Schang said. "A job like this may sound like paradise after you've spent forty years piloting starships of every size and description, but let me tell you, Kirk, I'd gladly switch places with you at the blink of an eye. Do you know what this job entails? It's talk, nothing but talk. I speak, a computer transcribes my words into symbols, another computer interprets those symbols back into words and tells people what I've been saying. We talk back and forth constantly, me and the computers, but I never actually do a damned thing. I miss being emperor of my own little kingdom with nobody looking over my shoulder. You've got the best job in the Galaxy, Kirk, and don't ever forget it."

"I try not to, sir, but calm has its blessings too."

"Well, you can have them. Give me a good healthy dose of action. I'm afraid I'm going to rot, sitting in this chair. Another year of this place and I'll be like a flower that nobody's remembered to water."

"Have you requested a transfer?"

"A dozen times. Ten dozen times. Requested. Asked. Pleaded. Begged. You're too valuable where you are, they tell me. I don't believe a word. Why do they need me? The computers could do it all—and they'd enjoy it."

Kirk tried to appear sympathetic. He knew Commodore Schang was deliberately exaggerating the worst aspects of his job. Commanding a starbase was a complex and arduous task. The decisions Schang was required to make might affect the lives of the millions of entities, human and otherwise, who resided in this sector of the Galaxy. If the job was boring, that was only because Commodore Schang performed it so well. If he hadn't, the excitement he craved would have arrived at his doorstep in a great wave.

"But you didn't come here to listen to an old man's senile prattling," Schang went on. "What can I do for you, Kirk? Somebody in the game room been cheating your crew at cards? One of the ladies make off with a man's life savings?"

"Nothing as dramatic as that, sir. I only wanted to see whether you had any orders waiting for me."

Schang looked puzzled. "If I did, don't you think I would have contacted you the moment you docked?"

"I only wanted to be sure."

"Mind telling me why?" Schang leaned back in his chair and let a satisfied smile creep across his face. "You've got some trick up your sleeve, Kirk. I know you too well. Tell me and, if you want, I can promise it won't go any farther than these four walls."

Kirk nodded. He knew he could trust his former commander's discretion. "I've been considering making a stop at a quarantined planet. There's been a report of a man living among a proscribed alien species."

Schang shrugged. "I don't see any problem with that. Enforcing Star Fleet directives is certainly part of your normal duties. Go to this planet, find the man, and arrest him."

"That's just it, sir. I may not want to arrest him."

Schang's eyes narrowed. "A friend of yours?"

"No, sir. It's the man's daughter. She's here on Starbase 13 and has been trying to locate him."

"Gilla Dupree," Schang said flatly.

Kirk showed his surprise. "You know about her?"

"Probably a good deal more than you, I'm afraid. Star Fleet Command contacted me concerning Miss Dupree. My orders were, if she located her father, to let them know at once. Has she?"

Kirk nodded reluctantly. "She was supposed to meet a man here, a trader named Merkle. He claims to have seen her father recently on a quarantined planet. She came to me to ask for help in getting there."

"Did she tell you the name of the planet?"

"Yes, but I haven't had time to run a computer check on it yet."

"Well, keep it to yourself. If I knew, I might feel obligated to inform Star Fleet Command."

"I appreciate that, sir."

"But what about this fellow, Merkle? Isn't he aware that it's a felony to land on a quarantined planet?"

Kirk smiled. "I was able to point that out to him

personally. He had demanded a rather large sum from Miss Dupree in return for his information. I convinced him to divulge what he knew for free—as a favor to me."

"And in return you promised not to bring charges against him. Neat, Kirk, very neat. Personally, though, I don't regard quarantine regulations lightly. A lot of traders, like Merkle, violate them in hopes of making a big score. When I catch them, I don't hesitate. If something's sufficiently wrong with a planet to warrant it getting declared off limits to all human contact, then there's always a good reason behind it." Schang leaned forward and stared fixedly at Kirk. "Are you aware of the identity of Gilla Dupree's father?"

"Should I be?"

"Why do you think Star Fleet Command is interested in the matter? Her father is Jacob Kell. Now do you know him?"

"Kell the traitor?" said Kirk, utterly astonished. Kell's name was a curse word throughout the Federation. Gilla Dupree's father? It seemed impossible to believe.

"Traitor may be too strong a term. Turncoat is more accurate. Kell left the Federation and went to live among the Klingons, but as far as anyone knows, he's never compromised his past loyalties. I knew the man fairly well at one time. He was a fine officer. Don't ask me to explain what went wrong with him. Space is a funny thing. It eats away at some men and leaves the rest of us untouched. Kell was a man who got eaten. Now, if Merkle can be believed, he's back among us again."

Kirk looked straight at Schang. "Do you intend to notify Star Fleet Command?"

"That depends on you. What are your intentions now that you know who you're dealing with?"

"The same as before. I'm going to this planet, find the man, and convince him to leave with Miss Dupree."

"Kell won't be easy to convince—of anything."

"And I won't be easy to refuse."

Schang nodded, stroking his chin thoughtfully. "All right," he said. "I trust you. I won't say anything. At least not until after you're well under way. And I can't tell anyone where you've gone. I don't know myself. I think you can handle Kell. If you can't, then nobody can."

"Thank you, Commodore. I appreciate this. If there was some way I could repay you for—"

Schang held up one big hand. "As a matter of fact, now that I think of it, there is something you can do." He grinned. "Jim, I need a favor."

"Of course, sir. Anything reasonable."

"I'm not sure I can honestly say it's reasonable. Here—I'll let you decide for yourself." He pushed a button on the side of his desk. A moment later, a door opened in the back of the office and a young man dressed in the uniform of a Star Fleet crewman sauntered through. He was thin, red-haired, and wore a vacant crooked smile. Without saluting either of the officers present, he sat down on a corner of Commodore Schang's desk. "Well, Dad," the crewman said, "is this the fellow you were telling me about?" His bored gaze slid quickly past Kirk.

"Albert," Schang said, "this is Captain James Kirk of the *Enterprise*. Jim, this is my son Albert."

"I'm—ah—pleased to meet you, Albert."

"Same here." Albert looked at Kirk more closely. "The *Enterprise*? Isn't that the boat with the warp drive?"

Kirk nodded tightly. The *Enterprise* was a starship; it wasn't a boat.

"See, Dad?" Albert said, swinging his attention

back to his father. "I told you I learned a thing or two at the Academy."

The expression on Commodore Schang's face could not have been more indicative of his acute discomfort. "Albert, perhaps you could leave Captain Kirk and I alone again."

"Sure, Dad. Whatever you say. You're the boss." Albert came to his feet and headed toward the door through which he had entered. He waved a casual hand. "Be seeing you, Kirk."

Commodore Schang concentrated on the bare surface of his desk. When they were alone, he looked at Kirk, his eyes reflecting his embarrassment. "Now you know my problem, Jim. Albert is my son, my only son. When his mother and I were divorced, she took him and raised him on Earth and I didn't see the boy for fifteen years. It was the usual story between us. She saw me once every fourth year and decided she wanted a full-time husband and father or none at all. I arranged for Albert to receive an Academy appointment. Aurora—my wife—told me he wanted it. Who knows? He washed out after less than a year and was reduced to crewman's rank. I pulled some strings and had him assigned here. He's not a bad kid. He just doesn't know a damned thing about anything and thinks he knows it all."

"Don't we all," Kirk said, "at one time or another?"

"I don't know. I've tried everything with him. Maybe it was my fault. Maybe he needed a father when he was growing up. That's where you come in, where I need your help. Take Albert under your arm. Teach him. Train him. Make a man out of him even if it kills him in the process."

"Me?" Kirk felt stunned. "You want me to take your son aboard the *Enterprise*?"

"I can have the orders in circulation within the hour—me and my computers."

Kirk tried to think quickly. "But I don't have an open position. My crew roster is full."

"Do you have a personal steward?"

Kirk shook his head. "I don't believe in servants. Not in this day and age." He was beginning to suspect that Commodore Schang had had this plan in mind all along. He was moving too swiftly for a man acting from impulse.

"Well, now you do. It's the perfect assignment for Albert."

"But, sir, I can't just—"

"As a favor?" Schang said softly. "For old time's sake?"

Kirk knew further resistance was hopeless. He shook his head wearily. "I'll do what I can, sir."

"That's all I ask. Albert and I have—ah—discussed this. If you hadn't come here on your own, I undoubtedly would have called you. Albert seems eager for the change. He tells me starbase duty is boring. It's the one area where he and I happen to agree."

Kirk came to his feet, sensing that the interview was over. "There is one other thing I'd like to ask from you, sir. The next time you see Albert, remind him that he's expected to salute officers. I don't want any bad examples set for my other crewmen."

Commander Schang grinned. "I get the feeling, Jim, that by the time you're through with Albert, he's going to know who sets the examples in this universe and who doesn't."

5

For Kirk, it was an exhilarating feeling being back aboard his own ship, free from the constraints of outside authority, rushing through the familiar void of interstellar space. He was reminded of an analogy Commodore Schang had drawn: the captain of a starship was like an emperor ruling his own limited domain. Is that me? Kirk wondered. But a benevolent emperor. I'm no tyrant, he reminded himself carefully.

Kirk sat in his command chair in the inner lower portion of the bridge. Directly in front of him sat Lieutenant Sulu, the chief helmsman, and Ensign Chekov, the navigator. Behind Kirk in the outer elevation of the bridge were the duty stations of the various technical personnel, including Lieutenant Uhura, the communications officer. Mr. Spock was not present on the bridge at this moment, but Kirk expected him shortly. He had asked Spock to relieve him an hour early, and Spock was as punctual as an atomic clock.

As he tried to do every few minutes, Kirk lifted his eyes and gazed at the viewscreen that covered most of the curved wall directly ahead. He looked at the stars, studied their patterns, then lowered his eyes. No sign of trouble—nothing untoward to be seen. Of course, the ship's computer would undoubtedly provide advance warning of any serious trouble ahead, but Kirk preferred to use his own eyes as an additional guarantee of safety. Computers rarely failed anymore, but it had been known to happen. It was the captain's responsibility to ensure the well-being of his ship and crew.

As happy as he was to be in space again, Kirk felt some regret that those irresponsible days of shore leave on Starbase 13 were over. He had enjoyed himself immensely, much as one part of him hated to admit it. So had a number of others. Upon returning to space, Kirk had found it necessary to convene two summary courts-martial, issue four immediate demotions, and write five severe reprimands for actions committed during the period of leave. Not that any of this had surprised or disappointed him. Kirk was well aware that the *Enterprise* was a miniature human society composed of 430 separate, distinct, and very human individuals. And I am the emperor, he thought once again. I am ultimately responsible for everything, good and bad, that goes on here. The glory and the burden are both mine to bear.

The soft, clipped tones of Ensign Chekov broke through his reverie. Kirk looked up. Chekov was talking to Sulu in the seat beside him. "So you really don't know why there are no Russian bears in Russian zoos," he was saying.

Sulu shook his head. "As a matter of fact, when I was a child, I visited Moscow with my parents. I'm sure I saw a bear in the zoo there."

"How do you know it was a Russian bear?"

"Well . . . I don't know. How do you know?"

"That's just the point," Chekov said. "If it's in a Russian zoo, then it isn't a Russian bear."

Kirk was smiling. Ensign Chekov sometimes showed a predilection for relating long, involved, often pointless but always entertaining stories.

Lieutenant Sulu sighed. "All right, Chekov, I'll bite. Tell me why there are no Russian bears in Russian zoos."

"Well, it's a long story."

"I rather thought it would be."

"In fact, it goes back nearly a thousand years to a time when Russia was ruled by a monarch known as Ivan the Magnificent, who should never be confused with Ivan the Terrible, although he was indeed terrible, or with Ivan the Cruel, although he was indeed cruel, or with Ivan the Dreadful, although he was indeed dreadful. The most dominant characteristic of Ivan the Magnificent was his extreme jealousy. He could not endure the thought of any other man possessing one thing that he himself did not possess."

"Then why wasn't he known as Ivan the Jealous?" Sulu said.

"Because his name was Ivan the Magnificent."

"Go on."

"Now in the lands ruled by Ivan the Magnificent there lived a young peasant named Pavel."

Sulu looked suspicious. "That's your name."

"A distant ancestor, but coincidentally, this Pavel happened to very much resemble me. He was kind, generous, intelligent, industrious, and very handsome. He loved a young girl named Natasha, who lived in the same village as he and who was said to be the single most beautiful girl in all of Russia. Fortunately, she also loved Pavel, and a day was established for their marriage."

"But what does this story have to do with bears?" Sulu asked.

"That part comes later. Now, as I said, Ivan the Magnificent was extremely jealous. So when he learned that Pavel was to marry the most beautiful girl in all of Russia, he began frothing at the mouth and determined that the bride must be his own. On the day of the wedding Ivan the Magnificent and a band of Cossacks attacked the village and carried Natasha away to Ivan's palace in a distant city. Pavel fought valiantly against the invaders, but the Cossacks were too numerous and well armed."

"I thought this was supposed to be about bears," Sulu said impatiently.

"It's not over yet, is it?" said Chekov. "Now this was also the winter of the Great Golden Comet, which as you will recall from an earlier story of mine is the reason why all polar bears have white fur."

"Ah," said Sulu, with satisfaction, "a bear at last."

"While many polar bears live in Russia," Chekov said stiffly, "not all polar bears are Russian bears, which is why you often see them in Russian zoos. In any event, because of the presence in the sky of the Great Golden Comet, it proved impossible for Ivan the Magnificent to marry Natasha until spring, for all his astrologers and soothsayers cautioned against the deed and Ivan the Magnificent, like most mean, cruel, terrible men, was very superstitious. Naturally, this proved especially fortunate for Pavel, who broken by despair had wandered aimlessly away into the forest, where for many days he had eaten only nuts and berries—and not many of these, since it was winter. Then one day he met a bear."

"What sort of bear?" asked Sulu.

"Why, a Russian bear, of course," said Chekov. "What do you think this story is about? And the bear growled and stood on its hind legs and made as if to eat Pavel, who in his despair did not resist or run or climb a tree or dig a hole with his hands in the snow. Such behavior puzzled the bear, who was accustomed to producing immediate fear in humans much like our—" Chekov glanced past his shoulder and lowered his voice "—much like our beloved captain. So the bear said to Pavel, 'Aren't you afraid that I will eat you? It is winter, when most bears are asleep and when if you meet a bear who is not asleep he is almost certainly going to be hungry, which as a matter of fact I am.' But Pavel just shook his head. 'I don't care whether you eat me or not.' He then went on to explain the whole story of Ivan and Natasha and his own deep despair. Now this bear, like all bears, was very sentimental beneath his fearsome exterior, much like our own—"

Kirk coughed meaningfully.

"Much like many people," Chekov said hastily, "and to show his sympathy, the bear promised not to eat Pavel. 'What I wish,' Pavel said, 'is that you could eat Ivan the Magnificent. If you did, I and all of my countrymen would honor you forever.' But bears are as realistic as they are sentimental and honor means little to them. 'Could you be more specific?' said the bear. Pavel thought for a bit and then said, 'I would guarantee that no Russian bear will ever again be slain by a Russian huntsman if only you would promise to make a meal of Ivan the Magnificent.'

"Now the bear, being a realist, wasn't about to fall for such a blanket assertion, but he did manage to extract from Pavel a less expansive promise to do what he could to ensure that no Russian bear would ever again be locked inside a Russian zoo. Since there were many more huntsmen than zoos in those days, that seemed a far more plausible guarantee.

'Tell me everything you know about this Ivan the Magnificent,' said the bear. 'He is undoubtedly well guarded in his palace, and since I have no safe way of getting there, if the diner cannot go to the meal, then some means must be devised for getting the meal to come to the diner.' Pavel told the bear everything he knew. He said Ivan was mean, terrible, cruel, and dreadful. He said Ivan's most dominant characteristic was his extreme jealousy. Then the bear had an idea. He told Pavel to stay where he was and hurried into the forest, where he visited all the caves in the neighborhood and woke all the bears who were sleeping. 'I am about to be married,' he proclaimed, 'to the most beautiful bear in all of Russia. You must come to the wedding. All the bears in the forest must come. I promise a glorious feast.'

"Now," said Chekov, "did I remember to mention how lucky Pavel had been in his aimless wandering? The fact is, he had managed to end up only a few short kilometers from the walls of the very city where Ivan the Magnificent made his home. Because of this, Ivan soon learned of the great wedding between the bears to be held in the forest. And he was jealous—extremely jealous. 'The most beautiful bear in all of Russia!' he cried jealously. 'That bear must be mine!'"

"But why?" Sulu said. "Surely, he didn't want to marry a bear."

"Not at all. He wanted to kill the bear and hang the skin—the most beautiful in all of Russia—upon his wall. So, on the day of the wedding, Ivan led a band of Cossacks into the forest, but the bears at the urging of the groom had secreted themselves behind trees and rocks, and as soon as Ivan and the Cossacks arrived, they pounced out and gobbled them up down to the very last button."

"And that's the end of the story?" Sulu said.

"Almost. Pavel was chosen to replace Ivan as monarch. He married Natasha, who bore him nine children, and reigned in peace and plenty for sixty-six years. And that's the end of the story."

"What about the bear?" said Sulu.

"I thought you'd never ask. The bear had his troubles. His compatriots were very angry with him. 'You promised us a wedding feast,' they cried. 'We got the feast but no wedding. Where is this bride of yours, the most supposedly beautiful bear in all of Russia?' And do you know what the bear said in response to this?"

"I can't possibly guess," said Sulu.

"He said, 'She's in a Russian zoo.' Get it? A Russian bear in a Russian zoo? Well, there are no Russian bears in Russian zoos and that was his way of saying there had been no such bride."

"Then Pavel kept his promise?"

"Of course."

Sulu was shaking his head. "Why do your stories always end this way?"

"What way?" said Chekov.

"Happily. In Japan our stories always end tragically."

"So do mine," said Chekov, "if your name happens to be Ivan the Magnificent."

Kirk felt a hand on his shoulder and turned. Mr. Spock stood beside the chair. "I'm prepared to relieve you now, Captain."

"Fine," said Kirk. "I've been waiting for you. Nothing interesting to report. Our present velocity: warp four. Estimated time of arrival: three days, fifteen hours. Mr. Chekov was telling us a story. A pity you had to miss it."

"I did arrive in time to hear the end."

Kirk stood and stretched as Spock assumed the command chair. "Perhaps Mr. Chekov will be kind enough to fill you in on the parts you missed."

"I'm afraid Chekov can't do that, sir," Sulu said. "He makes up his stories as he goes along and never remembers a word a minute after he's finished telling them."

Kirk shook his head and grinned. Chekov huddled close to his console, as if oblivious to the conversation around him. "It's your bridge, Mr. Spock," Kirk said, starting to leave.

"Oh, Captain?" said Spock.

Kirk paused. "Yes, what is it?"

"On my way here I met Dr. McCoy, who suggested that you might care to join him for dinner in the officers' mess."

"I'm afraid I'll be dining in my quarters."

"Alone?"

Kirk tried to suppress his irritation but succeeded only partially. "What concern is that of yours, Mr. Spock?"

"Regulations state that in the event of an emergency care should be taken to ensure that unauthorized personnel are not made aware of details beyond their own jurisdictions."

Kirk nodded tightly. Spock was right. "Miss Dupree will be dining with me. That does meet with your approval, I hope."

"I merely sought a necessary piece of information, Captain. I meant no offense."

"No, of course not, Mr. Spock. I'm sorry." Feeling suddenly very much like a tyrant, Kirk hurried to the turbolift, hoping to escape the bridge before he snapped at someone else's heels.

6

As the door to his quarters slid open, James Kirk turned in time to see the figure of Albert Schang come wobbling through the gap. Schang balanced a covered metal tray in the palm of each hand, and for a breathless moment it was an open question whether he would reach the safety of the table before losing what remained of his balance and letting both trays tumble to the floor.

Schang reached the table first. He deposited one tray in front of Kirk, swept around the table, and placed the other before Gilla Dupree.

Schang came languidly to attention. "Will that do for now, sir?"

Kirk nodded. If nothing else, these last few days had allowed him time to inculcate the rudiments of military courtesy into Schang. "You can uncover the trays for us."

"Oh, sure, Captain." Schang removed the lids from both trays, revealing two steaming plates of traditional Chinese cooking underneath. Kirk had personally chosen the vegetables from those produced in the hydroponic gardens. In deference to Gilla's religious beliefs, there were no meats.

"And bring the wine," said Kirk.

"Now?"

"Yes, now."

"But it's all the way back in the galley."

"Then I guess you're going to have to take a walk."

Schang frowned, started to say something else, thought better of it, turned, and went out. Kirk sighed. For years he had stoically endured the hardships of shipboard life without the aid of a personal steward. Now that he had one, he knew he had been right all along. Not that Albert Schang was a typical steward. Most captains would have clapped the man in irons long before now.

Gilla gazed at the food in front of her, smiling tentatively. "This does look good. And what's this?" She held a pair of wooden stalks between her fingers. "It's been years since I've used chopsticks."

"Do you want me to show you how?"

"No, I think I remember."

"Then maybe you'd better show me. I'm afraid it has been a while."

The door slid open and Schang stepped through, a small plastic tube clutched in the fingers of one hand. He deposited the tube in the center of the table and looked at Kirk. "Anything else, sir?"

Kirk shook his head, glad to be rid of the man. "You can go."

"Well, ring if you want me. I'll be in the crewmen's mess. My dinnertime too, you know."

"Salute me," Kirk said automatically.

"Oh, sure. Sorry." Schang raised his hand limply, swung on a heel, and went out.

Kirk watched him go, shaking his head, then reached out and picked up the tube. He shook it gently, pried open the cap with a thumbnail, and held it tilted over Gilla's glass. A thick milkish fluid dripped slowly out. "How much do you want?" he asked, as he poured.

"Only a little, please. I haven't drunk anything alcoholic in so long it worries me."

He let the fluid cover the bottom of her glass, then poured an equal amount in his own. "Give it a minute," he said. "It should expand in the air." Even as he spoke, the fluid in both glasses was beginning to fizz noisily. "It's the best vintage we have on board. Not from Earth, of course, but they say the factories on Ossium IV are nearly as good."

Gilla's glass was half filled with an amber liquid. She raised it to her lips and sipped tentatively. "It's excellent," she said, laying down her glass. "In fact, that's part of my problem. I love a good wine, but as a Jain, I have to regard the grape—even the artificially constructed variety—as a relatively high form of life."

"Oh, I'm sorry." He looked at her plate—tomatoes, beans, water chestnuts, pieces of onion, peppers. If a grape was a higher form of life, what were these? He felt a sinking sensation in his stomach. "If you'd rather not eat . . ."

"Oh, no." She laughed tenderly, easing his worry. "I didn't mean to imply that. A meal like this is perfectly fine for me. As long as someone else cooks the food—commits the act of murder—then it's acceptable for me to eat the dead husks. If it wasn't, we Jains would soon starve to death en masse."

"I understand," Kirk said.

"Do you?" She smiled. "No, you don't. But I don't really expect anything else. My religion is a very old one, and much of it seems to make little sense in our modern world. To me, it's not the literal dictates that matter: it's the view of existence, the philosophy of life, that lies behind them. I believe that a reverence for all forms of life, even the wind and the rocks, is a tremendous thing for a person to possess."

"I can't argue with that," Kirk said. "But I notice that you're not wearing that surgical mask anymore."

"A literal dictate," she said. "And it tends to get in the way of communicating with people. I think that's important too."

"I know you do."

"How?"

"From your work. You forget. No artist is ever a stranger to anyone familiar with his or her work." Kirk drank his wine and toyed with his food. Gilla, using the chopsticks like a practiced hand, ate more quickly.

"Anything else?" Kirk said, when he saw that she had finished. "I could get us some dessert."

She shook her head. "I'll just finish the wine." She patted her stomach under the table. "I feel stuffed." She wore a long white gown similar to the one she had worn at the starbase. "That was delicious."

"It was good." Kirk finished his own meal. "We'll be reaching our destination shortly. I know you must be looking forward to seeing your father again, but I wish we had time for another dinner like this."

"I wish the same thing." She smiled. "But what about you, Captain? Are you looking forward to seeing my father?"

"I don't understand. Should I be?"

"I know that by now you must be aware of his identity. I'll bet the commander told you back at the starbase. Kell the traitor. I believe that's how he's known. Do you intend to arrest him?"

"I don't know," Kirk answered honestly. "That will depend upon the situation. As far as anyone knows, Kell has never violated the Federation's trust."

"Do you know why he went away?"

Her question caught Kirk by surprise. "Why, no. Can anyone explain that, except Kell himself?"

"I can."

"Then . . . then would you?"

"My father was involved in an accident. He was the captain of a large starship, one almost as large as yours, and he and two of the science officers under his command had taken a shuttle from the main ship to investigate a quasarlike object several parsecs away. Apparently, what happened was that the intense gravitational force of the object damaged the shuttle. The communications systems were destroyed and a severe leakage developed in the fuel reserves. My father made some calculations and determined that the shuttle at its present mass could not possibly reach the ship."

"Did he try to jettison?" Kirk said.

"Yes. He threw out everything on board and calculated again. He was still short—by slightly more than two hundred pounds. In terms of travel time, that meant several hundred thousand kilometers. Even that close, he wouldn't be able to call the main ship. My father weighed two hundred pounds. He put on a suit, which he had saved for just such an eventuality, and went out the lock."

"He was stranded," said Kirk. It was the fate dreaded by every man who had ever served in space. "How long did it take for help to come?"

"Twenty-seven days," she said. "The navigational instruments aboard the shuttle proved to be damaged as well. The two science officers never reached the main ship. Only through a bit of freakish luck were they found at all."

"Nearly a full month," Kirk said. He tried not to show his horror. Alone in the vastness of the void with no company except the stars, strong men had gone irrevocably mad in much less time than that.

"He was never the same after that. He wasn't crazy. He had survived by savoring his isolation, reconciling himself to total sensory deprivation. The result was, when they found him, he could no longer endure the close contact of another human being. It made him physically ill. He quite literally had to be alone. The doctors tried to cure him. They failed. In the end, he felt he had no choice. He resigned from Star Fleet."

"And did what?"

"At first he tried to live with me. Naturally, I left him alone as much as possible. He became a prisoner in our apartment. Eventually, it got so he could feel the presence of others through the walls. It made him sick."

"That must have been a dreadful experience for you."

"I suppose it was. I honestly never thought of it that way. He was sick and I wanted to help him but I couldn't. The Klingons heard about his condition. I don't know how. I suppose they monitor our channels. An agent visited my father and made him an offer. If he would agree to forsake the Federation, the Klingons would give him an M-type planet of his own and sufficient means and materials to survive."

"And he accepted," Kirk said, unable entirely to disguise his distaste.

"He refused," she said flatly. "He knew what their motivation was: the Klingons wanted to use him for their own propaganda purposes. I made him change his mind. I begged and pleaded and forced him to say yes. I knew, if he didn't go, he'd kill himself. For a Jain—and I was already practicing the faith— suicide is an ambiguous act. If done through slow starvation at the end of one's natural life, it is regarded as a beneficent way of dying. Suicide by violence, for selfish ends, is murder of the worst sort. I didn't want him to do that."

"Why has none of this ever been made public?" Kirk said.

"Can't you guess? Would the Federation want to admit there were good and sufficient reasons for my father choosing to live among the Klingons? They treated him horribly. They never gave him a chance to live a productive life. They broke his will and then ignored him. It must have been a terrible embarrassment. So they branded him a traitor and let it go at that. I tried to correct the picture. No one would listen to me."

"Have you heard from your father since he went away?"

"Not directly, no. A diplomat helped me—a friend. He told me my father had left the Klingon Empire. They had lied to him, as he had known all along they would. The last few years, I've been trying to find him. And now I have."

"On NC513-II. Heartland."

"Yes."

He looked at her carefully and then reached for the wine. She made no objection as he filled both glasses. "Give me a minute," he said, "and then I'll tell you about the place."

"I'd like to know," she said.

"And I'd like to tell you."

7

James Kirk and Gilla Dupree sat shoulder to shoulder on the small couch that occupied one corner of Kirk's private quarters. Turning slightly, they brought their wine glasses together and let them touch. "Now tell me," Gilla said, after they had drunk. "What is this planet like? Heartland. Isn't that an odd name for an alien world."

"All I can tell you is what the ship's computer told me. Heartland is the aliens' own name for their planet. They call themselves Danons. Only a few hundred are known to exist. They all live in a single village. The Danons are among the oldest intelligent races ever discovered. Eons past, they occupied large portions of the Galaxy and may even have visited Earth in prehistoric times. When their civilization fell, they returned to their original home-world—Heartland. Now they are close to extinct. Heartland itself is an M-type planet, with large oceans, vast forests, and considerable natural vegetation. Forty years ago—with the permission of the Danons—an attempt was made to establish a human colony in the area close to the native village. Within a year the effort had to be abandoned. Everyone in the colony had gone mad."

"How bizarre," she said. "But—why?"

"It was never determined. Disease was suspected, but no evidence of biological infection was ever found. The colonists themselves could provide no help. None ever recovered. Heartland, naturally, was placed under a strict quarantine. By going there your father has violated a Federation edict."

"Do you think that matters to him? Or me?"

"No, but it doesn't explain why he went there."

She shrugged. "I have no idea."

"Then I suppose we'll just have to ask him." Kirk stood up, draining his glass. "Speaking of going places, could I interest you in a walk? There's a place on board ship I'd like to show you. I'm certain you'll like it."

She gazed up at him, tilting her head, smiling. "Where? I thought I'd seen all of the ship—except those places your security men won't let me enter."

"Have you visited the herbarium?"

"No. What's that?"

"I'd rather show you." He took her hand and helped her stand. "It's not far."

Before leaving, Kirk rang for Crewman Schang, who appeared shortly, chewing a mouthful of food. "I'll be in the herbarium with Miss Dupree. I don't want to be disturbed unless it's an absolute emergency. Do you understand?"

"Sure, Captain."

"And you can clear the table while I'm gone."

"I wasn't completely through with my own dinner yet."

"You'll have to finish later."

"There won't be any later. They're shutting down the mess for this shift."

"Then next time eat faster."

Kirk led Gilla out of the room. While they waited for the turbolift, she said, "That steward of yours seems a bit sullen."

Kirk laughed. "He's new on board. But he's learning."

She got a knowing look in her eye. "With you as a teacher, I'm not surprised."

"Is that supposed to be a compliment?"

"I'm not sure. I get the impression, Captain Kirk, that you can be a most frightening man when you want to be."

"Me? I'm as meek as a lamb." They rode the horizontal turbolift.

"A lamb, perhaps, but one with very sharp teeth. I think your steward would agree with my evaluation."

The herbarium was Kirk's favorite room aboard the *Enterprise*. As soon as they entered the area and the doors cycled shut behind them, they stopped and stood frozen. The herbarium was a garden of Earthly—and alien—delights, where a thousand varieties of plant life grew untamed. Gilla made an eager, excited sound deep in her throat and hurried down the dirt path. Kirk, following at a more sedate pace, found her crouched at the foot of a broad rhododendron. She held up her hands cupped together. "Look. I caught a butterfly. It's black with orange spots. The most beautiful thing I've seen in years."

"And real too." He crouched beside her. "Not a hologram or a construct. But aren't they common on Earth?"

"I don't live on Earth anymore. I left when Father did and went to Luna. I try to keep a small private garden. It's nothing compared to this. Look. Even the sky is blue."

"Well, that's paint," he said. The combined scents of the numerous flowers threatened to overwhelm his nostrils. A gentle artificial wind whipped through the trees, brushing Gilla's long hair.

"The ancients thought that the sky was painted. Does it matter that they were wrong then and right now?"

She opened her hands. For a moment the butterfly stood revealed in its splendor perched on the palm of one hand, as still and mysterious as the void. Then, suddenly, wings flapping, it flew up and away. Sweeping across the path, it came to rest upon the naked bud of a buttercup.

Kirk stood, brushing the soil from his trousers. "See? I said you'd like it here."

"Oh, I do. It's so intensely private. I can see why cooped up for months aboard a ship you'd find it a tremendous luxury. Doesn't anyone else ever come here?"

"They can, but few do, except for the biologists, and they're more concerned with collecting samples and doing research than relaxing with the wonders of nature."

"I don't understand it. I could stay here forever."

Without thinking, Kirk reached for her. His hands went around her back and he felt the bony ridge of her spine. She raised her chin, eyes shut, and waited for him.

The communicator at his belt emitted a loud beep.

Kirk stepped back. "Damn it," he said.

Gilla laughed. "The eyes of the gods are observing us, Captain."

"For the sake of whoever's calling, it had better be something like that." He put the portable communicator to his lips and said, "Captain Kirk here."

"Mr. Spock, Captain. I apologize for the interruption, but your steward told me where to find you."

"Yes?" said Kirk, trying to keep the irritation out of his voice.

"Mr. Scott from the engine room has reported the possibility of engine malfunction. We appear to be losing velocity."

"What does the computer say?"

"Negative, Captain."

"Then it's not likely anything serious."

"No, but I thought you should be informed."

"You did the right thing, Mr. Spock." If anything serious did develop, he wouldn't want to have to explain later what he was doing in the herbarium during the emergency. "I'll be right up in a few moments."

"As you wish, Captain."

It wasn't as Kirk wished. He refastened the communicator to his belt and turned to look at Gilla. "Duty calls," he said simply.

She smiled sympathetically. "I'll wait here."

"I may not be back for some time. I'm sure there's nothing drastically wrong, but I'll have to wait until the problem's located and corrected."

"I have nothing else to do." Leaning forward, almost lunging, she let her lips brush his cheek. "And I like it here."

Her kiss—as perfunctory as it might have seemed —went straight to his head. As Kirk marched to the bridge, he felt as if he were walking on top of the wind.

8

Captain's Log, Stardate 4246.7:

Upon our arrival at Heartland, I ordered my helmsman to place the ship into orbit around the planet. An immediate full sensor scan of the surface will commence as soon as a stable orbit is achieved. From the viewscreen, Heartland appears to be as reported: a lush M-type planet, with large oceans and considerable continental vegetation, an excellent prospect for human colonization. While here, I intend to investigate the question of continued quarantine and make a recommendation upon our departure. Our passenger, Gilla Dupree, remains under observation in sick bay. The exact nature of her illness—if any —is as yet undetermined.

"Anything to report, Lieutenant?" said Captain James Kirk, swiveling his command chair so that he faced the lean dark figure of his communications officer, Lieutenant Uhura. She sat before her console in the outer elevated section of the bridge.

"No, sir. I'm continuing to send the message you

requested at two-minute intervals. There's been no response."

"Well, keep trying. Mr. Spock?" Kirk swiveled his chair again. "What can you tell me?" Spock stood in front of the hooded screen of the library/computer station.

"Heartland appears to be among the more habitable planets in the Galaxy. I have already cataloged close to seven hundred major indigenous forms of life."

"The atmosphere?" said Kirk.

"As reported. A perfect eighty-twenty nitrogen-oxygen mix."

"Any indications of intelligent life besides that one known village?"

"No, Captain. Nothing."

"Then it would appear most likely that Kell is living there."

"It would appear so, yes."

"Do you have a population figure for the village?"

"I'm getting it now as a matter of fact." Spock leaned close to his console. "One hundred nine bipedal forms," he said, standing straight again.

"One of whom could be Kell?"

"Yes. The figure, of course, is not exact."

"But it still seems low. Tap the computer. See if you can obtain a figure for the time of the colony."

"I already have that, Captain. At the time of the establishment of the human colony on Heartland, the indigenous Danon population was four hundred fifty-seven."

"Then they appear to be continuing to lose population."

"Yes, Captain."

"And that severe a decline in only forty years would tend to indicate that final extinction cannot be far off."

"Barring a revival, I would say so, yes."

Kirk nodded. He knew he was only speaking his thoughts aloud. "Continue with your work, Mr. Spock."

The turbolift doors slid open. Kirk turned to see Dr. McCoy entering the bridge. He came directly across the room and stood beside Kirk's chair. "Anything interesting, Jim?" he said, gazing at the big viewscreen and its panorama of the planet beneath them.

"Nothing that we didn't expect. The Danon population has fallen from four hundred to one hundred in the past forty years."

McCoy whistled softly. "That barely leaves enough for a stable breeding base. Someone at Star Fleet Command ought to be interested in that."

"I hope so," said Kirk. "I'd hate to have to come all this way on my own authority and bring back nothing."

"Then you haven't found Kell yet?"

Kirk shook his head and indicated Lieutenant Uhura. "We're calling the village at two-minute intervals. If he's there, he's not answering."

"Should he? I understand he doesn't like people."

Kirk looked curiously at McCoy. "Then Gilla told you the story too."

"Yesterday. I'm glad she did. All these years I've regarded Kell as a terrible traitor. Now I think I understand the man a little better."

"I've had Uhura mention Gilla in her broadcasts. I thought that might flush him out if nothing else does."

"What if it doesn't? Then what do you intend to do?"

"We'll have to beam down to the village and look around for ourselves."

"And if he isn't there?"

"Then we're in trouble." Kirk pointed to the viewscreen. "It's a big planet."

A thick mass of dark clouds obscured a quarter of the larger northern continent. McCoy said, "That looks like snow."

"It's winter in the north."

"But the Danon village is in the south?"

"Close to the equator. The weather is probably pretty mild all year round."

"That's even more of a reason for Kell to be there. When you do beam down—if you do—make sure you leave a spot in the landing party for me."

"You? Why?" Kirk was somewhat surprised. McCoy rarely volunteered for such duty, leaving the decision whether a doctor was necessary up to Kirk.

"Because if what happened to the colonists happens to you, you're going to need a doctor. Mass psychosis is no joke."

"No evidence was found to support a biological cause."

"I'd still prefer to be with you. Heartland is an alien planet, no matter how pretty it looks up there on the screen. There's nothing that says it has to obey our expectations."

Kirk couldn't dispute that. "You're welcome to come, Bones. But what about Gilla? Is it safe to leave her yet?"

"I've ordered her released from sick bay." He turned and glanced at the turbolift doors. "In fact, I expect her here any minute."

"Then there's nothing wrong with her?" Kirk couldn't keep the relief out of his voice. In the three days since he had returned to the herbarium and found Gilla Dupree unconscious, he had not known a moment free from worry.

"I saw no further reason to keep her under observation, no."

"Then it was just another fainting spell?"

"Yes," McCoy said, a certain vagueness in his manner. "It was a faint."

Kirk looked at him suspiciously. "And what else? You're holding something back on me, Bones. I can tell."

McCoy laughed and put a hand on Kirk's shoulder. "Jim, damn it, don't be silly. You know how we doctors are: hard to pin down. There's nothing wrong with the woman. She's perfectly fine."

"Captain Kirk?" said a voice from behind.

He turned his chair. Lieutenant Uhura was motioning to him. "Are you getting something?" he asked.

"I think so, sir. A signal. It's very vague."

Kirk stood up and crossed the room. McCoy followed. "From the village?" Kirk said, standing behind her chair.

"No, but it's close. I'm trying to pinpoint—" Her hands moved at the console. "Ah, I think I have it now." There was a burst of static. She nodded. "That's it, but he's not broadcasting."

Kirk leaned over. "Here, let me try to talk to him."

Uhura turned a dial on the console and flicked a switch. "All right, sir. Go ahead."

9

Kirk spoke into the console: "This is Captain James T. Kirk of the U.S.S. *Enterprise* speaking. Please identify yourself and state the reasons for your presence on Heartland."

The voice that answered could be heard dimly through the continuing static. It was a man's voice, though high-pitched, almost shrill. "*Enterprise?* Did you say *Enterprise?* What's that? A ship?"

"I asked you to identify yourself. Are you Kell? Jacob Kell?"

"Who? Speak louder. I can't hear you."

Kirk tried to slow his voice down. "Jacob Kell. Are you Kell?"

A burst of laughter came from the console. All at once the static faded, and the voice could be heard distinctly. "I'm Bates. Reni Bates. Who the hell is Jacob Kell?"

Kirk glanced at McCoy, who made a puzzled face and shrugged his shoulders. "Mr. Bates," Kirk said, "what are you doing on Heartland? Are you aware that the planet was placed under Federation quarantine forty years ago?"

"I've been here that long, Captain. Longer. I've

been here close to forever. Heartland is my home."

Spock, who had joined the group around the console, said softly, "The man appears to be claiming to be one of the original colonists."

"Is that possible?" McCoy said.

"Anything's possible," said Kirk. "We'll have to run a computer check. There ought to be a listing of the colonists who came here and another of those who were later evacuated."

"I'll see to that now, Captain," said Spock. He hurried off to the library/computer station.

"Of course," McCoy said, "it might actually be Kell. He could be lying."

"But why? If it is Kell, he didn't have to answer our signals." Kirk leaned close to the console again. "Mr. Bates, can you tell me something about yourself? How did you come to arrive on Heartland? How old are you now?"

"Old?" Bates laughed again, a mirthless sound, at least on the radio. "Don't ask me something like that, Captain. They took the clocks and calenders when the crazy ones went away. Day and night is all I've got, Captain. The sun goes up and the sun comes down. I don't count the times it happens."

Kirk looked at McCoy. "He's familiar with what happened to the actual colonists."

"Kell might be too."

Kirk nodded. Spock was continuing to work at the library/computer station. Kirk decided to try another tack with Bates. The computer would eventually tell him everything he needed to know about the man's origins. "Mr. Bates, are you certain you know nothing of a man named Kell? Are you the only human on Heartland? Do you know of another one?"

There was a long pause before Bates spoke again. Kirk could sense his hesitancy. "Is Kell a big man?"

he said. "A big man with big hands and a bald head?"

"That sounds like him, yes," said Kirk.

"Well, then he's here. I didn't know his name. I wasn't trying to lie to you."

"I believe you, Mr. Bates."

"He's with the Danons."

"In the village?"

Bates chuckled at some private joke. "That's the only place you'll find any Danons."

Spock came hurrying over. "I checked the rosters as you requested, Captain, and the name Reni Bates does appear on the list of colonists."

"Was he evacuated?"

"No. When the rescue party arrived, he was missing. A search was conducted but nothing was found. Bates was presumed to be dead."

McCoy nodded thoughtfully. "As we agreed earlier, it's a big planet."

Kirk turned back to the console. "Mr. Bates, I want to ask you if—" A wave of static poured from the receiver, forcing Kirk to fall silent. The static increased in volume and changed into an angry roaring howl of noise. Kirk grabbed his ears. The noise suddenly ceased.

"Damn it," said Kirk. "He's cut us off."

"It may have been a transmission failure, sir," Uhura said, working frantically at her console with no apparent result. "The signal was very weak to begin with."

"No wonder," said McCoy. "His radio was forty years old."

"Was that my father you were talking to?"

Kirk turned in surprise. Sometime during the course of his conversation with Reni Bates, Gilla Dupree had entered the bridge. She stood glaring at him, her eyes angry. It was the first time he had seen her awake since he had left her in the herbarium more than three days ago. He moved toward her. "Gilla, are you all right?"

She regarded him coldly, her posture rigid. "I'm perfectly fine. But I asked you a question, Captain. Was that my father?"

Kirk halted his advance. "No, it was another man calling himself Reni Bates. He may have been left over from the group who tried to colonize Heartland forty years ago."

"Has he seen my father?"

"He says he has, yes."

"Where?"

"In the Danon village."

"Then we must go there. At once."

Kirk looked at her suspiciously. She seemed to be under a great strain. Her whole body was wound up tight as a spring. Kirk glanced at McCoy, but the doctor refused to meet his eye.

"We probably will go there," Kirk said. "Eventually."

"I want to go now."

"Captain, may I offer a suggestion?" It was Spock.

"Yes, of course." Kirk welcomed the respite from Gilla's inexplicable hostility. "Say whatever you want."

"In my opinion, our wisest course would be to speak directly with this man Bates before attempting to enter the alien village. If Bates has actually lived on Heartland for forty years, he'll be in possession of information that cannot be found in the few official reports at our disposal."

Kirk nodded. Spock had done nothing but voice his own thoughts aloud. He wondered if Spock was aware of that too and had done it deliberately—to deflect some of Gilla's anger toward himself. "I happen to agree with your evaluation, Mr. Spock. We'll do as you suggest."

"And my father?" said Gilla, her voice rising sharply.

Kirk tried to be diplomatic. "If your father is in the Danon village, he won't likely be going anywhere. Something on this planet managed to drive close to one hundred people insane forty years ago. I have a responsibility to know as much as possible about what I'm getting into before risking the lives of my crew."

"I'm not a member of your crew, Captain."

"But you are under my authority. I'll expect you to obey my commands."

The anger in her eyes grew more intense. She stood stiffly, hands clenched at her sides, apparently debating whether to speak. At last, without another word, she turned sharply and headed toward the turbolift. The doors slid open and she stepped through. A moment later, she was gone.

"Don't let that worry you," McCoy said reassuringly. He came over and stood beside Kirk. "She's not really angry at you."

"If she isn't, she gave a damn good impression."

"She's worried. And frightened. I know—I talked with her about it earlier. She's been scared to death it would turn out that her father wasn't here after all, and she'd have to start the whole search procedure over again."

"But I told her he was here. That should have made her happy."

"Not necessarily. She hasn't seen him yet. Neither have you, for that matter. All we have to go on is what Bates said, and Bates didn't even know Kell's name. Wait until we know for certain. She'll be better then."

"I hope you're right. For her sake." Kirk turned, moving swiftly into action. "Lieutenant Uhura, I want you to pinpoint Bates's exact location and relay the data to the transporter room. Mr. Spock, contact Mr. Scott and have him report to the bridge immediately. Dr. McCoy, you'll probably want to check in at sick bay. There's no telling how long we may be gone."

During the brief flurry of activity that gripped the bridge, Kirk slipped away to his command chair. He tried to take an interest in the geography of Heartland as shown on the viewscreen ahead, but his thoughts kept returning to Gilla Dupree. Damn that woman anyway. Didn't she have any idea what it meant to be responsible for the lives of more than four hundred people?

"Jim, I think there's something else we ought to discuss."

Kirk looked up at Dr. McCoy, surprised to find him still present on the bridge. "Sure, Bones, what?"

"I gather that you're intending to beam down to the planetary surface in the very near future."

"As soon as possible, yes."

"Will Gilla be included in the landing party?"

Kirk shook his head. "It'll probably just make her angrier at me, but no. A planet with as many unanswered questions as Heartland is no place for a novice."

"I think you ought to reconsider."

Kirk was surprised. If anything, because of her fragile physical condition, he had expected McCoy to argue strongly in favor of leaving Gilla behind. "Would you mind telling me why, Bones?"

"It's my medical opinion, Jim. I think the best thing we could do for Gilla now would be to give her the opportunity of seeing her father as soon as possible."

"You talk as if it's a matter of extreme haste. What's the hurry, Bones?"

"I just think it would be for the best," McCoy said. "Take my word for it. After all, I am the doctor, aren't I?"

McCoy hurried away toward the turbolift, leaving a puzzled Kirk behind.

10

As soon as he reached the surface of Heartland, his body materializing at the edge of a wide lake, his toes actually touching the water, Kirk drew his hand phaser and began a cautious turn designed to acquaint him with the specifics of his new environment. According to the sensors, Heartland possessed few forms of life large enough to present any probable physical danger, but this was still an alien planet, where nothing could ever be taken for granted.

After completing the full circuit of his turn, Kirk returned his phaser to his utility belt and beckoned the other members of the landing party to join him. He had brought a total of seven with him. They had arrived in two groups—the transporter could handle no more than six human-sized bodies at a time—and now stood scattered at various places along the lakeside. Everyone appeared to have landed in good health. Besides McCoy and Spock, Kirk had picked three other men well able to take care of themselves in emergency situations: Lieutenant Sulu and a pair of security guards, Mosley and Doyle. The seventh member of the *Enterprise* crew included in the party was Albert Schang. Kirk hoped he hadn't made a mistake by bringing him here. Teach him and train him, Commodore Schang had said of his son. Well, Kirk knew of no better way of training a crewman than dropping him down on an alien planet and seeing how he behaved himself. It was the Star Fleet version of the old medieval trial by ordeal.

The final member of the landing party was the result of a last-minute decision by Kirk. In the end, as a result of Dr. McCoy's continued urging, he had chosen to let Gilla Dupree accompany them here.

She was the first of the group to reach Kirk's side. "Do you think that's where he lives?" she said, pointing to a small, well-constructed log cabin not far away. Kirk had noticed the cabin during his initial inspection of the area.

"All we can do is stick our heads inside and see what's there."

"I wonder how much he knows about my father."

"Not a great deal, apparently. We'll have to question him. He may know enough to give us some idea of your father's probable reaction to our visit."

"You mean he may not want to see me at all."

"I was thinking more of us than you, but considering his past mental state, it's possible even that is true."

"I should have thought of that myself instead of just wanting to go charging down here."

"You were eager to see him. And worried. I understand that."

"I still should have thought things out more fully." He knew she was trying to make amends for her anger on the bridge, and he accepted her apology as such. The remaining members of the landing party had joined Gilla and him by now.

McCoy was gazing at the log cabin. "Not a sign of life anywhere," he said. "It almost makes a person feel unwelcome."

"Well, Bates didn't exactly invite us down to lunch."
Kirk had the group spread out in a line before advancing on the cabin. "Keep your phasers in your belts but don't forget they're there. This man hasn't set eyes on another human being—except possibly Kell—in forty years. There's no telling what sort of mental state he might be in."

Kirk kept his eyes fixed on the open doorway as the eight of them drew close to the cabin. The sky was a flat pure shade of blue, unmarked by clouds. The temperature was mild, the air dry. There was no appreciable breeze.

A man stood in the cabin doorway. Kirk had to blink twice to be sure he was seeing what he thought he saw. The man—Reni Bates?—wore a knee-length tunic made from animal hides. As Kirk watched, the man stepped forward into the light. He was short, skinny, and stooped. His face was very old but the eyes remained bright. His beard and hair—what remained of it—were cloud-white.

Kirk stopped a few meters in front of the man and raised a hand, halting the others. "Bates?" he said. "I'm Captain Kirk."

"You got here quick enough." His voice was soft but tight, betraying no obvious emotion, but Kirk was nonetheless sure of one thing: this man was very afraid of something. Kirk felt he could almost smell the other man's fear.

He tried to assume a relaxed, unthreatening posture. His voice, when he spoke, was deliberately smooth and friendly. "Are you Reni Bates?"

The old man hesitated, eyes darting, as if seeking an avenue of escape. "I'm him. Who sent you here?"

Kirk shook his head and smiled. "No one sent us." He dropped to the ground, sitting on his haunches, and waved at the others to do the same. After a moment's deliberation, Bates also crouched down. A sitting man, Kirk knew, was always less threatening than a standing man. "We've come to try to locate this man Kell."

"I told you he was in the village." Bates's suspiciousness did not go away. "What did you come here for?"

"We wanted to talk to you first. You've been here more than forty years. There must be a lot you could tell us. About the planet. About Kell. About these aliens—the Danons."

Bates's manner stiffened even more. "What about the Danons?"

Kirk tried a smile. "That was what we were hoping you could tell us."

Bates looked back past his shoulder, as if expecting to find an eavesdropper there. "I stay away from them." He waved at the cabin. "This is my home. I don't go around the village. I mind my own business and you ought to do the same."

"But you will talk to us, won't you? You will help?" Gilla had joined them. Her voice was pleading.

Bates looked up and his eyes grew large. "Who . . . ?" He shifted his gaze nervously back to Kirk. "Who's she?"

"This is Gilla Dupree. Kell is her father."

"And I want to see him very much," Gilla said. "Is he all right? When was the last time you saw him?"

Bates stood up and took a step backward. For a moment, Kirk thought that they had lost the man entirely. Then he pointed to the cabin door. "Why don't we go in there and talk about it? I'll tell you what I can."

Kirk followed Bates into the cabin. The floor of the single room was covered here and there with furs. Bates sat down on one pile and tucked his legs beneath him. A moment later, Gilla Dupree entered the cabin. She sat with Kirk on another pile.

Bates said, "You'll have to excuse my manner, Captain. I get few visitors here. You're the first person I've talked to in more than forty years."

"What about my father?" Gilla said.

Bates looked away. "I'm afraid I haven't really had a chance to say much to him." His voice was soft, almost a whisper. Kirk was beginning to understand at least a part of Bates's nervousness. Gilla was a woman. The chances were, Bates hadn't seen anyone else like her since the abandonment of the colony.

"You must have had a very lonely life," Gilla said sympathetically.

Bates nodded sorrowfully. It was clear that Gilla at least had gained a measure of his confidence. "I suppose you could call it that. I have a few tapes and books to keep me entertained." He nodded toward a wooden crate in one corner. "I hunt and fish and gather food in the forest. And I have my own thoughts. That's not bad company, once you get used to it. And there's Lola."

"Lola?" said Kirk.

"My piker."

"What's that?" Gilla said.

"That there is a piker." Bates pointed to what Kirk had taken to be just another pile of furs, but as he looked more closely, he saw that this one was moving, breathing. He peered more closely and discovered a pair of brown eyes gazing back at him. "A piker is a lot like a dog except that they live longer. Lola's been with me since the day I arrived here. I suspect she'll still be here long after I'm gone."

Gilla got up and went over to the animal. Crouching beside it, she stroked the beast's fur. It made a noise like the purring of a cat, but much louder and more guttural. A piece of the fur swung back and forth on the floor. The tail was wagging.

"How about that?" said Bates. "Lola likes you. Before the others went away, Lola used to chase after them tooth and claw. I was the only human she'd let within forty feet of her. Lola's older now, I guess. Hell, so am I."

"Bates," said Kirk, seeking to take advantage of the old man's reverie to redirect the conversation into a more meaningful course, "why didn't you leave Heartland when the others did?"

Some of the suspiciousness returned immediately to his face, but as he continued to observe Gilla and the piker, it softened and became less openly hostile. "They were crazy and I wasn't. Why should I have left?"

"But the ship missed you. How did that happen?"

"I was out hunting. Lola was with me. I never even saw the ship land. When I came back, everyone was gone."

"Weren't you surprised?"

"Not really." Bates paused before answering each of Kirk's questions, as if he was using the time to compose his replies in advance. "I knew something was going to happen. They were crazy."

"But why them and why not you?"

Bates shrugged with calculated casualness. "I guess I was fortunate."

"And you don't know why it happened to them?"

The pause before his reply was the longest yet. "I think the Danons did something to them."

"What?" said Gilla, her voice anxious.

"I don't know exactly. I might even be wrong. It's just a guess, a theory of mine. I had nothing to do with any of it—nothing at all."

Kirk was sure he was lying, but he saw nothing to be gained by pressing the point. "And how is Kell? If your theory is correct, he must be in danger."

"I don't think so. The last time I saw him he was fine."

"When was that?" Gilla said.

Bates shrugged. "Like I told you before, it's all day and night to me. Don't ask me anything about time."

"But you've never talked to him?" Kirk said.

"I never tried. You see, the first time I saw him was when his ship landed. I was kind of excited. It was the first time in . . . since the others left. I went to the village and tried to spy on him. He caught me watching. A big man, like I told you, with big hands. He chased me into the woods and hurt me." Bates tilted his head and pushed back a wad of stringy hair. A jagged scar three inches long showed on his scalp. "He hit me with a sharp rock."

"My father would never do that," Gilla said.

Bates looked apologetic. "Well, he did. It wasn't meanness. I suppose he had a reason. Maybe the Danons told him to. Maybe he didn't have any choice."

Kirk would have liked Bates to explain his last remarks more fully, but Gilla spoke first. "How many times have you seen him since then?"

"Oh, quite a few. I like to keep a pretty close eye on the village. It's a day's walk from here. I go over there and hide in the woods and watch what's going on. I'm pretty careful now and nobody's seen me. Once when I was there another ship landed, and a man got out and talked to your father for a long time. I don't know what they said. I couldn't get close enough to hear. After a while, the other man got back in his ship and left."

"That must have been Merkle," Gilla said to Kirk.

"Who?" said Bates.

"The man who told me that my father was here on Heartland." Gilla stood up. "Mr. Bates, I want to thank you very much for your help. I'm glad you've seen my father and that he seems to be all right. Now all I want to do is go to the village and talk to him for myself."

"I'd be willing to show you the way," Bates said slowly.

"Would you?" Gilla smiled radiantly. "I'd appreciate that very much, Mr. Bates."

Kirk did not attempt to interfere. If necessary, the transporter could be used to beam them back aboard the *Enterprise* and then down to the village again, but this might prove a better if slower way. The day's march would give them all a chance to get to know Heartland better. And, too, with Bates along, there was the possibility he might lose more of his reticence and reveal some of the things he was obviously choosing to conceal.

"I'll do it for you on one condition," Bates said, looking only at Gilla as he spoke. "You have to make me one promise."

"Of course, Mr. Bates," she said. "Whatever you want."

"I want you to promise not to listen to those things—those Danons. All they do is lie and lie and lie. They'll tell you anything. Don't listen to a word they tell you. Will you promise me that?"

She nodded with a solemnity that matched his. "You have my word of honor. All I want is to find my father. I want nothing else."

Bates seemed satisfied. He stood up and headed toward the door. As he did, the piker—Lola—stood too and followed him, a walking ball of shaggy gray fur. Scrambling to his feet, Kirk hurried in pursuit of the strange old man and his pet.

11

The Danon village rose up suddenly out of the forest, an unexpected island of mud-and-grass huts in a sea of greenery.

Kirk raised a hand, ordering the others to stop. He studied the village cautiously, failing to find the slightest indication of life within. The air was utterly silent. Even the familiar forest noises which had accompanied them the past day were now stilled.

Kirk turned to Spock, who stood behind him. He paused in surprise. There were only seven people in the party, not eight. Someone had vanished. "Bates?" he said. "What the hell happened to Bates?"

Spock seemed surprised too. The eyes of the others darted into the underbrush, but Bates failed to appear.

"He was walking right beside me a minute ago, sir," Crewman Schang volunteered. "Him and that big animal. I'd swear it."

"Gilla, did you see anything?" said Kirk.

She shook her head impatiently. Now that they had actually reached the village where her father probably resided, much of her anxiety had returned.

Kirk shrugged. "Well, we can't worry about him now. We'll have to go on without him."

"Go on where?" McCoy said. "For all the life that place shows, it might have been abandoned a thousand years ago."

"Maybe everyone's asleep," Sulu suggested.

"In the middle of the day?" said McCoy.

"Maybe that's when they sleep on this planet," Kirk said. "All I know is it's not doing us much good standing here arguing about it. We're going inside."

"Phasers out, sir?" Mosley asked. He was one of two red-shirted security guards, a big, tight-lipped man with a heavy red scar over his left eye.

"No. But keep your hands close. We have no idea what we're going to find in there."

The landing party—all eight of them—moved forward, approaching the nearest cluster of huts. These buildings, like the village itself, seemed placed without purpose or conscious design. Gilla hurried forward until she walked at Kirk's side. The strain on her face was obvious. He tried to comprehend the depth of her feelings. In a few more minutes, she might well be seeing her father again for the first time in years.

Kirk studied the first hut they passed. It wasn't large—the flat roof barely reached the level of his own head. No windows were visible, and the open doorway was barely broad enough for a man on his hands and knees to squeeze through. Kirk tried to peer through the gap. It seemed pitch dark inside.

Suddenly, there was movement in the doorway. Kirk halted and let his hand drop toward his belt. The others had seen the motion too. They also stopped.

A stooped figure emerged through the doorway and stood upright in the dust.

Kirk stared. His jaw went slack from astonishment. This must be a Danon, he realized.

The creature was naked—a male—and barely a meter tall. Its smooth skin was a gentle copper color. The head contained two narrow black eyes, a pair of broad flat nostrils, and a thin lipless mouth. The skull, like the body, was hairless. A pair of slightly curved horns perhaps three inches long protruded from the back of the head. The creature had a tail. It reached nearly to the ground and had a barbed tip at the end.

Kirk couldn't control his wonder.

The creature was an exact replica of Earth's most dreaded legendary being.

The Danon was a devil.

It never moved. Its eyes were focused on Kirk and stayed there. He shook his head in an effort to break the spell.

"Ask it about my father," Gilla said from beside him. "Find out what it knows."

Kirk made an attempt. "Kell?" he said. Clearing his throat, he tried again. "Can you tell us if Jacob Kell is here?"

There was absolutely no response from the Danon.

"It can't understand you," Gilla said.

"Bates said they all could."

"Kell is my father," said Gilla, speaking directly to the Danon. "Can you please tell me where to find him?"

Still, nothing.

Kirk touched her arm. "Maybe we ought to go on." He looked at the others. "We're going to keep looking. Come on."

They left the Danon where it stood. Two huts loomed ahead. Kirk moved between them. As he did, two more Danons emerged, one from each hut. Both were also males. It was difficult to tell them apart. Again, Kirk stopped.

"Ask them," said Gilla.

He did, turning first to one Danon and then to the other. He received no more response than he had before.

"I think they're deliberately playing stupid," Dr. McCoy said. He spoke in a soft voice, nearly whispering.

"Maybe they have a reason," Kirk said. "Maybe they have a leader whose job it is to talk to strangers like us."

"Then they could at least tell us how to find him. Or are we supposed to look for the one wearing purple robes? The prince among devils?"

Kirk shook his head. "I don't think that's the wisest way of regarding these creatures, Bones."

"It's hard to do otherwise. I'm not a superstitious man, but these things give me the willies."

"Try to control yourself." Kirk removed the portable communicator from his belt and tried to reach the *Enterprise* bridge. The chief engineer, Lieutenant Commander Scott, had assumed temporary command in the absence of Kirk and Spock. He answered the call.

"It's good to hear from you, sir," said Scott, his voice thick with the burr of his native accent. "Have you reached the alien village yet?"

"Just a few moments ago, Scotty. We've met the Danons but so far they won't talk with us."

"Then you haven't found Kell?"

"Not yet, but I have a feeling he's here. In any event, I want you to stand by to beam us back aboard as swiftly as possible if I signal you."

"Are you anticipating trouble, sir?"

"Not necessarily. It's only a precaution."

"The transporter room has your coordinates. I'll see that they're alerted."

"Fine, Scotty."

"Can you tell me what these Danons are like, sir?

I've been studying the reports and they sound like an interesting bunch."

"Oh, they are, Mr. Scott. They most definitely are."

"Sir?"

"I'll tell you all about it later, Scotty. There isn't time now."

"As you wish, Captain."

Kirk waved them forward. As they moved deeper into the village, the same pattern was repeated. Every time they passed a hut, a single Danon emerged from inside. All were adults, most were males, and none said a word. Kirk no longer attempted to communicate with them. He maintained a steady pace, refusing to pause, hopeful that his patience in the end would prove greater than theirs.

The monotony of huts and Danons was at last broken when they reached the center of the village. Here in a broad open space stood a high tower made from mortared stone. The tower was probably twenty meters tall, and the upper portion was formed in the shape of the capital letter Y, with the addition of a horizontal bar placed across the open top. The base of the tower was apparently hollow. There was an open doorway level with the ground.

Kirk walked up to the tower and looked inside the doorway. The room within was empty and dark.

He turned to the others, folding his arms across his chest. "We'll wait here," he said.

"Wait? Wait for what?" said Gilla. "We haven't found my father."

"I think we ought to give him a chance to find us."

"And if he doesn't?"

Kirk shrugged. "Then I guess we'll try another plan." He sat down in the dust and patted the ground beside him. "Care to join me?" he said.

12

The Danons began to gather almost at once. They appeared from all sides of the village and started to form a circle around the clearing. As more arrived, the circle grew wider, three and four deep in some places. Seen in such numbers, the Danons seemed even more alike than ever. They showed no obvious signs of aging, Kirk realized. There were no children but no old ones either.

"I count nearly one hundred," Spock said. "Wasn't that the sensor estimate of the Danon population?"

"It looks like they've all come out to give us a hearty welcome," said Kirk.

"It's not very hearty when they don't even bother to say hello," McCoy said.

"What are we going to do?" said Gilla.

"Just what we have been," Kirk said. "Sit and wait and be patient. I don't know what they're up to—if anything—but don't let them think you're spooked. If Chekov were here, I'd get him to tell us a story."

Kirk knew himself how difficult it was to follow his own advice. He might not be spooked, but he was disconcerted. Surrounded by a circle of one hundred devils. This must be what it's like in hell, he thought. Maybe when you arrive, they give you a hearty welcome there too.

"What's that?" said Sulu, pointing.

Kirk followed the line of his finger. Then he saw it too. Beyond the circle of Danons, a disembodied head floated in the air. It was a man's face, and it was moving toward them.

"Gilla, look," he said, touching her arm.

She turned and looked and sprang instantly to her feet. "Father!" she cried, stepping forward.

"Wait," said Kirk. He stood and caught her wrist. "Not yet. Let him come to us."

The circle parted as Kell came through it. He was a huge giant of a man, as big as he was broad. Powerful blue eyes blazed in the sockets of a high-domed head. There was something rigid and incredibly intense about the man even from a distance.

"He looks old," Gilla said.

"It's been a long time since you last saw him."

Kell halted in the dirt a few meters short of where they stood. He looked at each of them in turn, his eyes brushing quickly past Gilla and coming to rest on Kirk. "What the hell do you want here?" he said curtly.

"Father," said Gilla, her voice tender.

Kell's gaze never wavered from Kirk. "I asked you a question, Captain. I'd appreciate a reply."

"We brought this woman to see you. She's your daughter, Kell. Don't you recognize her?"

"I know her, but I don't believe you. No Star Fleet captain is going to bring his ship all this way on an errand of sentiment." He turned to Gilla at last and his manner immediately softened. "Why did you have to come here? How did you know where to find me?"

"A man told me. A trader named Merkle. He said he'd seen you here."

"That traitor." Kell spat violently. "I told him if he ever talked I'd kill him." He swung his gaze back to Kirk. His eyes were filled with bitterness and rage. "Do you find that amusing, Captain? Me, Kell, calling another man a traitor? I thought I was the archetype of the entire breed."

"I don't know about that, Kell. Your reputation, deserved or not, is none of my business. I do know that your presence on Heartland is a violation of the Prime Directive. This planet is quarantined by Federation edict."

Kell threw back his head and laughed wildly. "You and your Prime Directive can both go to hell for all I care. Listen here, Captain, don't you know anything? Don't you know I sold out the Federation years ago? Well, if I did, then I owe it nothing. Heartland is my planet. I make the rules here. I'm the law, not you, not the Federation." His eyes blazed with fury.

Kirk stood his ground calmly. "You chose to come here, Kell. This is Federation territory. You're expected to obey the law the same as any other man."

"Is that what you call it? Federation territory?" He swung an arm, pointing behind. "Why don't you tell that to them? The Federation is a petty, insignificant blot on the pages of cosmic history. When your ancestors were squatting in caves, the Danons had conquered one-half of the Galaxy. Don't tell me about your law, Captain. Tell it to them."

"You're a human being, Kell. They're not."

"You mean I was. I relinquished that privilege long ago." He thumped his chest with a fist. "I'm Kell. This is my planet. These are my people. Now get off my world."

With crisp military bearing, Kell turned on a heel

and marched toward the circle of Danons. Like Bates, he was dressed in a tunic of animal hides, but on him the garment looked almost new.

"Father!" cried Gilla, lunging forward in pursuit.

Kirk held her arm. "No. Not now. Let him go. Let him think—"

She spun on him, her arm swinging, and slapped him firmly on the face. "You drove him away! You and your threats! You and—and—!"

She faltered, suddenly staring wide-eyed at her own hand. She fell forward against Kirk's chest. He put a soothing arm around her shoulders.

Beyond Gilla, Kirk saw the grinning face of the devil.

It was one of the Danons.

"Ah, Captain, greetings, greetings." The Danon spoke with perfect clarity. Its head bounced on its shoulders with each word. "I am Dazi. Our village, our planet, all this is yours. Come. You need rest. We will bring food." The Danon gestured toward the village.

Kirk looked back at the others. Spock raised a quizzical eyebrow. McCoy shrugged.

"Where do you want us to go, Dazi?" said Kirk.

"To your hut. Two huts. As hosts, we provide food, comfort, and shelter."

"That sounds like the best offer we've heard all day," McCoy said.

Kirk nodded thoughtfully. Gilla clung to his arm. He told the Danon, "All right, show us the place. It looks like we're going to be staying here for a while."

The Danon grinned.

13

Dazi the Danon guided Kirk and the other persons from the *Enterprise* to a pair of huts at the opposite end of the village. Kirk placed Gilla in Dr. McCoy's care. Her eyes were glazed and she had not yet spoken. McCoy sat down on the ground beside her and began fumbling with his medikit. Kirk asked Dazi to explain what exactly was going on.

The Danon grinned its toothless grin. "These huts are for your shelter and comfort, Captain. If you require more, please state a need and immediate delivery will be made."

It was difficult to reconcile the alien's apparent friendliness with its satanic appearance. "Well, of course, we're all hungry," Kirk said. He glanced at Gilla and McCoy. "And we could probably use some blankets. Furs, if that's all you use."

"Food and warmth will arrive instantly." Dazi bowed and started to wheel away.

"And one other thing," Kirk said. "I'd like you to tell Kell where we're staying. If he wants to see his daughter again, she'll be here."

"Oh, Kell knows that—he does." This time, ducking its head, the Danon made a successful exit. Kirk stared after the creature, watching its barbed tail weaving in the air.

"What do you think it meant by that, sir?" Sulu asked.

Kirk shook his head. "Your guess is as good as mine. Mr. Spock, let's see exactly what we have here."

Dropping to his knees, Kirk squeezed through the doorway of the nearest hut. The place was empty inside, the floor made of hard dirt. There were no windows, but enough light managed to enter through the thin walls to allow adequate vision.

Kirk turned and looked at Mr. Spock, who had followed him inside. "We'll have to split up into two groups. I'll take this hut and you can have the other. McCoy and Gilla can stay with me. You take Mr. Sulu and Schang. We'll divide the security guards. Do you have a preference?"

"Both are competent professionals, Captain."

"Then I'll keep Mosley with me. He's easier on the nerves than Doyle."

"I'll go over now and inspect the other hut if you don't mind."

"No. There doesn't seem to be anything else to see here."

Kirk followed Spock out of the hut. Outside, while Spock went off to investigate the second hut, Kirk approached McCoy. Gilla lay on the ground with her head in his lap. Her eyes were shut and she seemed to be sleeping.

"I gave her a sedative," McCoy said. "She ought to be all right when she wakes up."

"Was it shock?"

"More or less." There was an angry look in McCoy's eyes. "How else could she react the way that man treated her?"

"It must have been quite a shock for him too, Bones."

"Did he act that way?"

"No, I suppose he didn't."

"Then let's feel sorry for her, not him."

Kirk reached for his belt. He unfastened the communicator, opened the antenna grid, and tried to call the *Enterprise*. When Scott answered, Kirk described the events of the past few minutes. "Dazi promised to bring us food and other necessary supplies. For the moment then, we'll sit fast here and see what develops."

"Do you think Kell will agree to go with you willingly?"

"I'd have to say the prospects don't appear too good."

"Then will you be using force?"

"I honestly don't know, Scotty. I need to know more about the local situation before deciding that. Kell has the Danons on his side. That's one factor that has to be considered."

"You said they didn't appear to be dangerous, sir."

"That's true, but appearances, as we all know, can deceive. Bates has lived here for forty years. He ought to know the Danons better than anyone. And he's frightened to death of them. I'm sure of that. And he must have a reason. I don't think it's because of their looks alone."

"Devils, huh, sir?"

"The spitting image, Mr. Scott."

"What a consternation it would cause in my native land, a superstitious place at best, should I appear in the streets with one of those creatures at my heels. I'll tell you, though, Captain, that if certain people saw me in such company, it would only confirm past suspicions concerning my character."

Kirk feigned surprise. "Why, Scotty, I never realized you'd led such a dissolute youth. In the officers' mess I've heard open speculation regarding how you manage to keep your angel's wings concealed under your uniform shirt."

"I must thank you and the other officers for that kind testimony, Captain. Are there any further instructions at this time?"

"No, I don't think so. Maintain your present orbital position. If there's trouble, I'll call you."

"It'll be night there soon, sir."

"We'll try to sleep. If nothing develops, I'll contact you in the morning."

"Fine, sir."

"Kirk out."

As Kirk was attaching the portable communicator to his belt, Spock emerged from the opposite hut. Kirk divided the landing party into the two prearranged groups, then helped McCoy carry Gilla into the hut. Crewman Mosley followed them inside.

A few moments later, Dazi reappeared, followed by five other Danons. Kirk waved them into the hut. The first four carried large earthen pots, which, when opened, proved to contain an assortment of fresh fruits and vegetables, the same types the landing party had eaten during their trek through the forest. The fifth Danon was laden with an armload of furs.

"I'd like to have my other men fed too," Kirk said.

Dazi was grinning, nodding his head. "Already accomplished, Captain. No problem." He shooed his companions out of the hut and made a quick exit in their wake.

"An efficient bunch," McCoy said drily. He dipped his fingers into one of the pots and pulled out a round orange fruit. He took a bite and smiled. "And good too."

Kirk and Mosley sat down to eat. When he'd had his fill, Kirk stood and announced that he was going outside to check on Spock and the others. Gilla was still asleep. McCoy had covered her body with one of the furs.

As he crossed the ground between the huts, Kirk glanced at the sky, which now showed a violent shade of reddish gold. The sun in the west hugged the green horizon. Darkness could not be more than fifteen or twenty minutes away.

Spock, Sulu, Schang, and Doyle crouched in a circle upon various furs. Four earthen pots sat among them. Doyle and Schang were still eating. As Kirk came through the door, he could hear Sulu's voice relating a story, the point of which seemed to be the reasons why there were no Japanese bears in Japanese zoos. As soon as he saw the captain, Sulu fell silent, grinning sheepishly.

Kirk pointedly ignored his lieutenant's plagiarism. "It's going to be dark shortly, Mr. Spock. Is there anything else you require for the night?"

"The Danons have us well-supplied, Captain. I'm sure the men will find a way of keeping themselves entertained." He glanced meaningfully at Sulu.

"I'll want you to keep a watch throughout the night. I know that makes it hard for anyone to get much rest, but we'll be doing the same in my hut. If there's any indication of trouble, don't hesitate to use your communicator."

"Are you expecting anything in particular, sir?" asked Doyle. He was a younger man than his colleague, Mosley, but more intelligent and no less competent. In the enlisted men's quarters, Doyle was known as a compulsive gambler, especially at cards, but unlike most of that type, he rarely lost.

Kirk shook his head. "I just want to be sure we keep alert. The Danons seem more than friendly, but I don't want that taken for granted."

"It won't be by me, sir. I've seen all kinds of aliens

in my life, but this bunch gives me the definite creeps."

"You shouldn't let appearances color your judgments, Doyle."

The man looked genuinely puzzled. "I don't think it's that, sir."

"Not because they look like devils?"

"Devils?" Doyle's confusion seemed to grow, then suddenly he smiled in apparent understanding. "Oh, them. Like on Earth, you mean. In the Christian religion."

"Don't you know what devils are, Doyle?"

"I know what they are, sir, but I didn't remember what they looked like. I was raised in the Rigellian system, you see. My parents were strict Morganites."

"And the Danons still give you the creeps?"

"Yes, sir, I guess you could say they do."

Kirk nodded thoughtfully and went back to his own hut. Inside, he found that Gilla was now awake. She was sitting up and gnawing at one of the fresh fruits. She looked at Kirk and smiled somewhat uncertainly. "I believe I owe you an apology for my behavior, Captain."

Kirk shook his head and sat down across from her. "No, not at all. I understand what you must have been going through."

She held up her hand and looked at it. "Perhaps you do but I don't. For a Jain to strike another human being is a terrible thing indeed."

"I wasn't harmed."

She bit her lip. "I'm not sure if that's the real point, Captain."

McCoy came noisily to his feet, stretching languidly. "Time to exercise the old legs before darkness sets in," he announced. "Mosley, how would you like to join me?"

"Me, sir?" said Mosley, stunned by the honor.

"There's something in the color of your skin I noted earlier," McCoy said. "I think we ought to go out in the sunlight where I can examine you better."

"But isn't it getting dark, sir?"

"Only the more reason for us to hurry." McCoy knelt down by the doorway. "Come along, Mosley. This could be serious."

When he was alone with Gilla, Kirk grinned. "One thing you can say for Bones: he's not subtle."

"Did I get the impression he thought you and I ought to be left alone?"

"It does seem possible." Kirk moved closer to her. "I just wanted you to know that I don't think the way your father treated you was very fair."

She shook her head. "I wish I could be as sure of that as you say you are, but I think it's at least partially my fault. I never really considered him, you see. It had become such an overwhelming obsession with me. I knew I wanted to find him, but I never bothered to think about what he wanted."

"Give him time. I'm sure seeing you was a shock for him."

"Did he seem shocked to you? I thought he was just angry."

"He was wrong."

"No." Her voice was soft; she spoke haltingly. "I'm wrong. He's right. The past is the past. My coming here was my way of trying to alter that fact, and it just can't be done. When I was a child, I loved him very much, and when he left, I missed that love and I wanted to have it again. I should have learned to treasure the memory. That was my error. If anyone should be aware of the inevitability of time's passage, it's a Jain. I'm supposed to have perspective. I'm supposed to realize the insignificance of worldly things."

"A fly is an insignificant, worldly thing," Kirk said,

"but to you its life is precious. I think you're wrong in what you're saying."

"I appreciate that, Captain."

"Jim."

"What?"

"You always call me Captain. My name is Jim."

She smiled, not without some embarrassment. "Jim," she said softly.

"I'm starting to get very afraid, Gilla." He reached out, touching her arm. Beneath the thin fabric of the gown, her flesh was cold.

"Afraid? What of?"

"Afraid that I'm falling in love with you."

She started to laugh but the sound stuck in her throat. "No," she said solemnly, "don't do that."

"What if I can't help myself?" He let his fingers circle her wrist.

"You have to. You must." She broke free of his grasp and came to her feet.

"Why? Is there something wrong with me?"

She turned her back so that he couldn't read her face. She shook her head. "I don't want you to be . . . hurt."

"Why?"

She shook her head.

"Is there someone else? Another man?"

"No." Her voice was hollow.

He stood up and started to move toward her. Suddenly, she turned. Her face was like a mask. "Jim, I wish you'd go. I don't want to talk to you— talk about it—anymore."

He stopped, uncertain whether to proceed. "Are you sure?"

She nodded. He thought her eyes were moist. "I'm positive."

14

Outside the hut, where darkness now held nearly complete sway over the land, Kirk found Dr. McCoy and Mr. Spock standing just far enough away so that there could be no suspicion that they might have been trying to listen in.

"We just left the other hut," McCoy said. "Crewman Doyle has managed to get a poker game organized. Our friend Dazi showed up and got roped into joining the game. So far, he's won two months' pay from Schang and another week's worth from Sulu."

"Maybe I ought to break that up before my entire crew goes broke."

"I wouldn't worry too much, Jim. I don't think Dazi has any concept of the value of money. Besides, Crewman Doyle might object to any interference. As near as I could tell, he seemed to be winning just about as much as Dazi. I tried to talk Mr. Spock into trying a hand but he refused. To a logical mind, poker must seem like a fool's pursuit."

"On the contrary, Doctor," said Spock. "Poker is extremely popular among Vulcans. The game is one of sublime logic, not blind chance. I chose not to join the game out of respect for the other players. I doubt that it would be possible for me to lose. Besides our ability to calculate odds swiftly in our heads, we Vulcans possess what is known as the perfect poker face."

McCoy grinned. "Now that I can believe." Totally serious, he turned to Kirk. "Is something the matter, Jim? You look dour. Is it Gilla? Her health?"

"No, she's perfectly fine."

"Then what is it?"

Kirk shrugged casually and tried to smile. "Just a touch of old-fashioned melancholia. It'll pass."

McCoy glanced at him carefully, his suspicion plain. "Well, at least you reminded me of my duty. I ought to go in and look at Gilla."

"I think I'll stay out here," Kirk said. "Watch the sun set."

"Fine. I'll see you inside, Jim, Spock."

For a long moment following McCoy's departure, Kirk and Spock stood in mutual silence, each lost in pursuit of private thoughts. Kirk tried to force his mind as far as possible from Gilla Dupree. Here on an alien world surrounded by presumably hostile forms of life was no place to start acting like a moonstruck puppy. Spock's presence helped ease his mind. Gilla spoke of the perspective of Jainism, but Kirk wondered what she made of Spock: the Vulcan was cosmic perspective personified, more like a rock than a man, a creature undisturbed by the raging emotions that so often distorted human vision. In certain respects, Kirk not only admired Spock; he envied him. It showed keenly in their friendship. With Spock, he could stand for long minutes—as he was now—without feeling the need to speak and make conversation. Even with as good a friend as McCoy, this was not always true. With Spock, silence served well when silence served best.

With his thoughts more in order—and some of his

melancholia eased—Kirk cleared his throat. "Well, Mr. Spock, you've been uncharacteristically reticent. What do you make of these Danons?"

"That's a difficult question for me to answer logically. The fact is that these creatures do disturb me."

"Could you be more specific?"

"Not so completely as I might prefer. I can only tell us this: as soon as we first entered this village, I received the distinct impression of the near presence of an extremely powerful mental force. Almost as soon as I recognized it, the force vanished. I did not feel it again until our meeting in the clearing with Mr. Kell. When he first appeared, I felt it once more, but again the impression was very brief."

"Why didn't you tell me about this before?"

"I wanted to be sure. I have now examined my own memory and have told you the parts of which I am certain."

"Is there more?"

"Only speculation. As you know, the mental powers of a Vulcan are considerably more advanced than those of a human. Something was definitely present on both occasions. I'd prefer to say no more at this time."

"You used the description 'mental force.' Did you mean telepathy?"

"Not necessarily, though it's possible."

"And this force was related to the Danons?"

"I'm not certain of that, no. What I felt seemed to be a separate entity, a vast, powerful, and incredibly ancient being."

Kirk rubbed his chin thoughtfully. "I haven't felt really at ease since we arrived here. Maybe I've sensed something of the same thing."

"That's certainly possible, Captain."

"Well, be sure to keep your ears—or whatever it

is you use—open. If you find out anything else, be sure to let me know."

McCoy reappeared and assured Kirk that Gilla seemed to be fine. The three of them then watched the final setting of Heartland's sun. In the clean cloudless atmosphere, the maneuver was a swift one, like a swimmer ducking beneath the waves. When it was over, Spock returned to his own hut and Kirk and McCoy crawled inside theirs. Gilla smiled as they entered. Kirk set up a portable lantern in the middle of the room. He and McCoy arranged the furs to make four beds. They ate some more of the fruit.

Crewman Mosley came back into the hut, shaking his head. "Those Danons are damned fast learners, sir," he told Kirk. "That Dazi took every credit to my name, and what it didn't get, Doyle took."

"Perhaps you've learned a valuable lesson," McCoy said.

Mosley's creased face broke into a grin. He winked. "There's always tomorrow, sir."

"You're a born optimist, Mosley."

"That too. But Doyle promised to loan me enough for a stake."

Kirk assigned two-hour watches. Mosley would start, to be relieved by McCoy and then it would be Kirk's turn. Gilla asked to be included, but Kirk refused her offer. When she started to argue, McCoy intervened.

"I think it might be wisest, Gilla, if you'd use these hours to get some rest."

"Are you sure that's necessary?"

"Doctor's orders."

She went off to her bed. Kirk lay down on his. With his eyes shut, distantly, he could hear McCoy and Mosley softly discussing the subject of poker. It seemed only a moment later when McCoy shook him awake. He stood his two-hour watch and then woke Mosley. He had trouble falling asleep again. When he awoke for the second time, it was to a loud noise in his ears. He turned over. The communicator he kept close to his head was beeping.

He sat up at once, grabbed the communicator, and flipped open the antenna grid. "This is Captain Kirk. What do you want? What's the problem?" He tried to shake off the aftereffects of slumber. McCoy was also awake, sitting across the hut with an anxious look on his face. Presumably, this was still his watch.

The flat dry tones of Mr. Spock reached his ears. "Sir, I'm afraid we may have some trouble."

"What is it, Spock?"

"Crewman Doyle, Captain. He's disappeared."

"Disappeared? What do you mean? Where did he go?"

"I'm afraid I have no idea."

"How long has he been gone?"

"I don't know that either. He apparently left the hut sometime during Crewman Schang's first watch."

"What does Schang have to say?"

"That seems to be the problem, Captain. Crewman Schang fell asleep. I only discovered his lapse a few moments before I called."

Kirk fought to restrain his temper. There was no use yelling—yet. He took a deep breath. "I'll be right over to talk with you, Mr. Spock," he said.

15

As Kirk led the remnants of his landing party through the Danon village, nothing stirred around them. The mud-and-grass huts they passed might well have been the dwelling places of slumbering ghosts or sleeping spirits for all the signs of life they showed. The air was totally silent. Even the wind had ceased to blow.

Kirk kept Crewman Mosley close to his side. In spite of their vastly different personalities, he and Doyle had apparently been close friends. Mosley was plainly worried. He moved with one hand resting on his phaser, and Kirk let him do it, trusting the man's professional instincts. Mosley said he held himself at least partially to blame for Doyle's disappearance.

"Why?" said Kirk. "You weren't even there when it happened. If anyone's to blame, it's Schang. He fell asleep on watch."

"But Schang's just a kid, sir, and I'm not. I should have seen what was happening. All the time we were playing cards, that alien kept talking to poor Doyle, whispering in his ear. I thought they were just discussing the game. But I know Doyle. He thinks he's a sly one. That alien told him something, tempted him, and Doyle fell for it."

"Then you think the Danons are responsible for his disappearance?"

"Don't you, sir?"

Kirk wasn't quite ready to answer that. He turned and looked back at those trailing him. Everyone was present: Spock, McCoy, Gilla, Sulu. Albert Schang brought up the rear. His anxious expression at least seemed to reflect a measure of shame.

When they reached the tower in the center of the village, Kirk stopped. At the foot of the structure directly in front of the open doorway stood the shell of a fire, ashes piled in the middle of a circle of smooth stones. Kneeling, Kirk passed his hand over the stones.

"It's warm," he said.

"Then someone was here last night," McCoy said.

"But where are they now?" Kirk stood up. "I think it's time to find them."

"You don't intend to go from hut to hut, waking each one individually?"

"I have a feeling they're not asleep. Mr. Sulu, Mosley. Start with the nearest huts. Peek inside. If you see a Danon—awake or asleep—ask it to please join us here. If you don't—"

"Just a moment, Captain. I think I see something." Spock stepped forward and went through the doorway in the base of the tower. A moment later, he reappeared with something in his hand: a bright red shirt.

"Doyle's," said McCoy.

Kirk took the shirt from Spock and examined it closely. The garment was not torn. There was no reason to believe it had been removed other than voluntarily.

"At least we know he was here," McCoy said.

"That's not the real question. I want to know where he is now."

"Captain." It was Spock again.

Kirk turned and looked where Spock was pointing. "Well, well," he said softly. "We seem to have company."

The Danons were arriving. The procession was almost exactly the same as the one the day before. As silently as mourners at a funeral, the Danons formed a circle around the clearing. Kirk waited until the last of them had arrived, then put his hands around his lips. There was no sign of Kell.

"Listen to me!" he called, turning in a circle to be sure that all of them heard. "One of my men has disappeared. I have reason to believe he was here with you last night. I want him returned. If he isn't, I won't be responsible for what occurs next."

The threat was a weak one and for all the response it immediately evoked, Kirk thought he might as well have saved his breath. Then one of the Danons broke from the circle and moved quickly toward Kirk. He recognized Dazi. The Danon was smiling.

"Captain, Captain, please," he said, like a parent addressing a miscreant child. "There is no need for senseless violence. No need at all."

"Then where is my crewman?"

"Why, with us," Dazi said, as though stating the obvious. "We have given him the best of care—only the finest."

Kirk kept a stony face. "Then bring him here."

"You wish to see the man?" Dazi seemed astonished.

"I do. And now."

The Danon's satanic features twisted into a frown of consternation. "All right, Captain. You are the boss." With a very human shrug, it turned and sped away, tail bouncing.

Dazi was gone for five minutes, perhaps longer. When he returned, he wasn't alone. Doyle was with him, clutching the Danon's hand. The two of them passed through the circle and approached Kirk and the others.

Doyle was naked. His eyes were vacant, his face a blank mask like that of a child seeing the world for the first time. As he walked beside Dazi, he wobbled on his feet, as though his body offered too great a burden to be easily borne.

Kirk walked toward them. Dazi stopped and so did Doyle. Kirk gazed straight into his crewman's eyes. There wasn't a hint of recognition there—not the slightest sign of life.

"Bones," Kirk said softly.

"I'm right here, Jim."

"You want to take Doyle and see what you can do for him."

"I'll try."

McCoy took Doyle's hand and led him a short distance away. Kirk heard Mosley emit a strangled cry. He turned and glared at the man.

"Get a grip on yourself. This is no time to lose your head."

"Yes, sir," said Mosley, his eyes filled with anger and disgust.

Kirk wasn't feeling especially calm himself. Doyle sat on his knees in front of McCoy. His lips were moving and he appeared to be speaking, but the sounds that emerged were sheer babble.

Kirk faced the Danon. "I want to see Kell. Now."

Dazi's wide grin had not faded. "Impossible to see Kell. He must sleep. Long, arduous night. Needs rest."

"You'll disturb him," Kirk said, biting out the words.

"Kell knows nothing. Cannot help. No doctor."

"Bring him here!" Kirk made no further effort to contain his rage. "And get those others out of here. I want to be alone with my own people."

For an instant almost too quick for the eye to

follow, Dazi's expression fluctuated. A look of utter contempt flashed across his face.

It was gone as suddenly as it had come. Dazi was smiling again. "As you desire, Captain. Kell will come."

He went away. Even before he disappeared into the village, the other Danons had begun to disperse. Kirk didn't bother watching them go.

"Anything for me, sir?" Mosley said, his voice tight with repressed emotion.

"No. Not now."

"We could teach them a lesson."

"How?"

"Burn a few of their huts."

"Petty revenge won't do any good. Nothing can change what's been done to poor Doyle."

Kirk noticed Spock standing off by himself, apparently lost in thought. He went over to him.

"An idea, Mr. Spock?"

"I felt it again, Captain."

"The mental force? When?"

"As you were talking with Dazi. It's been trying to keep itself concealed from me, but for that one instant, its barriers slipped."

"What did you find out?"

"Only that it seems to hate us. It may, in fact, hate everything. The emotion did not seem to be directed at any particular source."

"But you don't know what it is?"

"Not yet."

"You think you will?"

"In time, Captain, yes." Spock furrowed his brow. "If it lets down its guard again, I think I will."

Gilla Dupree came over to them. She asked Kirk, "Why do you want to see my father?"

"Because I'd rather try to talk with him than with Dazi or one of the other Danons."

"How can you be certain he knows anything?"

"Only two people have ever lived on Heartland for any length of time without going mad. One is Bates and the other is your father. Bates has disappeared. I want your father to explain to me how he's managed to be so lucky."

"You still don't trust him, do you?"

Kirk shook his head. "Do you?"

Seeing no other alternative, Kirk finally went over to Dr. McCoy, who was crouched on the ground beside Doyle, preparing a hypodermic. "How is he, Bones?" said Kirk.

"Not well." McCoy did not look up from his work. "I'm going to have to knock him out."

Kirk gazed at Doyle. His face was as barren as a blank slate. His eyes shifted in his head, darting senselessly from place to place. "He seems calm enough."

"For now, yes, but there's no way of saying how long that'll last."

"What's your diagnosis?"

"I haven't made one. He seems to have little or no awareness of his surroundings. I'd place his mental age at two or three. He's suffering from a severe psychosis. I don't know how it happened. I don't know how to help him."

"What do you recommend we do?"

"Transport him to sick bay for now, but I'm not equipped to handle extensive psychotherapy. Unless he improves soon, he'll need better and more permanent care eventually."

"An asylum."

"In his present condition, it's the only option."

"All right. I'll call Scotty and have him stand by."

"The sooner the better, Jim."

"I'll do it now." Kirk left McCoy to his labors and went over to stand beside the base of the tower.

Removing the portable communicator from his belt, he called the *Enterprise*. Mr. Scott answered. Kirk wondered if Scotty ever slept during his tours of temporary command. The example he set was almost too perfect to be endured.

Kirk explained why he was calling.

"Driven mad?" Scott said. "That's dreadful, sir. But how did it occur? Are these Danon creatures involved?"

"I'm sure they are, Mr. Scott, but I don't really know anything for sure. That's why I've asked to speak to Kell."

"I think that's a good idea, sir."

"I want you to have Nurse Chapel and three or four medics standing by in the transporter room. You'd better see that some security guards are on hand too. The shock of transport may snap Doyle temporarily awake."

"I'll see that it's done. Will you want a replacement sent for Crewman Doyle?"

"Not right away, no. I want to know more about what's going on before risking any additional lives."

"And your own, sir? Are you sure it's safe for anyone down there?"

"I'm not sure of anything, Mr. Scott. I'll talk to you later."

"Aye, aye, sir."

"Kirk out."

A heavy hand fell on his shoulder. Kirk turned to face the angry blazing eyes of Jacob Kell.

"Kirk, you fool!" Kell cried. "Didn't I warn you? Didn't I tell you to get off this planet? Now look what you've done. Look at that poor idiot. Are you satisfied? Are you proud of yourself?"

Kirk pushed Kell's hand away. "It wasn't my idea, Kell. You used to be an officer in Star Fleet. You must still retain some conception of the term *duty*.

What did you think I'd do? Pack up and go home because you growled at me?"

Dazi had returned with Kell. As the two men talked, the Danon skipped around them, its smile firmly in place.

"Look, Kirk," said Kell, his tone mollifying, "I didn't tell you anything that wasn't true. I warned you it wasn't safe for you to stay here. Are you trying to tell me I was wrong?"

"I'm saying that what you told me amounted to nothing. I can't ignore my duty on your say alone. It's really your decision to make, Kell. As long as you keep quiet and tell me nothing about what's going on around here, I'll have to stay and try to find out on my own."

"Can't you just—?" He turned and looked at Gilla. She had started to approach him but paused halfway, obviously uncertain whether to proceed. "Can't you just leave?" said Kell, swinging his attention back to Kirk. His voice was imploring, almost desperate.

"No," Kirk said flatly.

"Then—then—" Kell seemed on the verge of telling Kirk to go to hell, but something—perhaps it was Gilla—persuaded him to change his mind. "All right," he said in a voice laced with defeat. "Come to my hut and I'll tell you everything. But you've got to promise me. Promise that once you know, you'll leave here and take her—take Gilla—with you."

"You know I can't promise you that."

Kell shook his head. "I know." He turned away. "Come on."

"What about Gilla?" said Kirk. "Do you want her to come?"

"This doesn't concern her."

"Are you sure? She is your daughter."

His shoulders sagged. "All right. Tell her to come."

Kirk waved a hand at Gilla, who immediately came

running over to join them. As she came near, she looked at Kell and smiled and held out a hand. The diffidence she had shown toward him the previous day had vanished.

Kell looked past Gilla at Dazi. The Danon had stopped dancing. He stared back at Kell. Not a word passed between them.

Kell reached out, took Gilla's hand, and squeezed it in his. "It's good to see you again, Daughter," he said.

"And good to see you too, Father."

16

Seen from without, the hut where Jacob Kell resided resembled any other in the Danon village, but once he had actually crawled through the doorway and moved inside, James Kirk felt as though he had accidentally entered a different, more civilized world.

A window had been cut in the rear wall. A pane of glass—salvaged, Kirk assumed, from the ship Kell had used to reach Heartland—had been inserted in the gap. The floor of the hut was covered nearly from wall to wall with a thick soft red-and-gold carpet. Two metal chairs sat side by side near the back of the room, and there was a small wooden table, the top empty. Two paintings hung from opposite walls.

Kirk stood in the middle of the room and looked at the paintings. They were very similar—both depictions of the stars—though a closer inspection revealed that the stars shown were not nearly the same set. Both were genuine paintings of space. Not the sky—not what planet dwellers could observe any night they bothered to look, which was usually quite seldom—but space as seen, known, and experienced by those who lived within it. For a long moment,

Kirk let his gaze shift from wall to wall, painting to painting. The more he looked, the more he was affected. The paintings far exceeded the realism any photographer might hope to achieve: these paintings captured not only the substance of space but also its essence—its reality.

"Did you paint these?" Kirk asked, turning to Kell.

"While living among my Klingon friends."

"They're magnificent."

"Where do you think I got my artistic bent?" Gilla said. She now sat in one of the chairs, while Kell paced in front of her like a caged beast.

"I had a hundred more when I arrived here," Kell said. "I destroyed most of them with my ship. I kept these two. I don't know why."

Kirk stepped closer to the wall. Observing the painting from this near, he felt as if he were actually adrift among the stars. He made himself turn away at last, breaking the spell. "I recognize some of the individual stars but the constellations are unfamiliar."

"It's a view from space, not from a planet."

Kirk nodded and crossed the room to examine the second painting. Once again, he seemed to leave the real world far behind. He experienced the exhilaration of deep space vertigo.

"Now I understand." He faced Kell. "This is what you saw when you were stranded in space. You must have memorized every star."

Kell looked angry. "How did you know about that?"

"Gilla told me."

"You shouldn't have," he told her gently.

"Why, Father? Isn't it true? Shouldn't people know?"

"The truth was always there for anyone who wanted to look. No one cared. Ask Kirk about me. He'll tell you who I am: Kell the traitor. Kirk doesn't give a damn what pain I've had to endure."

"Why are you so intent on bearing that pain, Kell?" Kirk said. "Gilla told me what she did because she thought it was unfair for me not to know. Unfair to you—and unfair to the rest of us, too."

"What makes you think I give a damn what the rest of you think?"

"For one thing, these do." Kirk pointed to the paintings. "You can't get it out of your mind, can you?"

Kell smiled distantly. "Those paintings were done a long, long time ago. I was a sick man then. Did Gilla tell you that too?"

Kirk nodded.

"And haven't you noticed the difference? Tell him, Gilla. Tell him how it used to be. I couldn't be in the same room with another person without wanting to claw out my own guts."

"What cured you?"

He pointed to the floor. "Heartland did."

"Maybe you ought to explain."

"That's what you came here for, isn't it? Here, I'll start at the beginning. I came here in a Klingon ship—a shuttle. The trip took more than two years, Earth reckoning."

"Why did the Klingons let you go?"

"It wasn't their decision. I owed them nothing. They'd lied to me, given me none of the things they'd promised. I knew they would—knew all along." He looked at Gilla and made his voice sound more sympathetic. "But it was my own choice to make. I'm not blaming anyone. After my value to the Klingons had ended, they put me to work in their ministry of space exploration. It wasn't a military position. I told them I wouldn't touch anything like that. I worked in the archives. It was there that I came across a reference to Heartland. A Klingon ship had landed here five years before the first Federation survey team arrived."

"They made no effort to found a colony."

"That isn't what they were after. Not this close to the center of the Federation. They came to grab whatever they could take. There were a couple dozen Klingons in the ship. They discovered this village and moved in."

"What happened to them?"

"They went mad." Kell made a sound of disgust. "Klingons. What else could they expect?"

"That doesn't sound like much of a reason for wanting to come here too."

"It wasn't. Not at first. The reference simply intrigued me. Call it a mystery. I was bored. I undertook to find out more. Klingons rarely suffer from mental disorders. Unlike humans, they possess too many easily available outlets for their naturally aggressive impulses. They keep nothing bottled up inside to later go rotten. I learned about the Federation attempt to establish a colony on Heartland, and I learned that the colonists had all been driven mad. Eventually, I tracked down two survivors from the original Klingon mission. Both were still insane, confined to prisons. I spoke with them, and when I did, I realized they were making sense. It wasn't good sense but I discovered what had driven them mad. I took the shuttle and came here. The Klingons couldn't catch me. It's a big galaxy and they had no way of guessing where I was headed—or why."

"Then tell me," said Kirk. "Why?"

Kell grinned. "Because I'd learned that on this planet a man can become immortal."

Kirk stared at Kell for a long, astonished moment. The man's face was impassive; his eyes said he was telling the truth. "And are you?" said Kirk.

"Yes."

"Immortal?"

"I am."

"Perhaps you'd better explain."

"It's a matter of collective consciousness. The Danons are an old people. They've forgotten more about the nature of existence than you and I can ever hope to know. Each one of them is an individual entity. They are also something more, something greater."

"A mental force?" said Kirk.

Kell nodded. "You could call it that. A force that contains the essence of every Danon who ever lived. Something like that can never die."

"And you're part of it too?"

"Yes. And that's why I'm immortal. Oh, my body will eventually wither. It might take hundreds of years, but in time it won't be able to go on anymore. I don't care about the body. In here—" he tapped his chest "—in my soul, I can't die."

Kirk tried to keep an open mind. He didn't necessarily doubt anything Kell was telling him, but neither did he believe that it was the entire truth. Kell was holding back. He could sense that. "How does all this relate to what happened to Crewman Doyle? To the madness?"

"Because that is when the madness occurs. When an individual tries to enter the whole and fails."

"They go mad?"

"Always."

"But you didn't."

"I was fortunate. And strong. I had the will to succeed and I did."

"And Doyle didn't."

"The Danons are too kind. They understand the value of the gift they possess and do not hesitate to offer it to anyone. Learning to surrender one's individual nature, learning to exist as one component in a larger whole, goes against everything we humans —or Klingons—believe. The average mind simply cannot stand the strain. It snaps. I tried to warn Doyle. I told him of the danger. He wouldn't listen. Who can blame him? No one could have talked me out of it either."

"Did he have a choice?"

For the first time, Kell looked angry. "There's always a choice, Kirk. It's between life and death. Tell me: which would you prefer?"

"I imagine it depends on the circumstances."

"In this case, there are none. The Danons worship me. Before I arrived and entered the fusion, they were dying. They're an old race and much of their will to succeed has vanished. It's been years, I understand, since any last bore children. I was young and energetic. I've given the force a new sense of destiny —and the Danons too."

"But why, Father?" Gilla said. The hurt in her voice was plain.

Kell rocked on his heels and shut his eyes. "It's something, Gilla, that you cannot know until you've experienced it yourself."

"Are you soliciting her?" Kirk said.

"No!" Kell's eyes flashed angrily. But there was more there than simple rage: he was also afraid. "I want her off this planet as soon as possible."

"Aren't you acting rather selfishly? Aren't you willing to share your good fortune with the rest of us?"

"Don't misunderstand me, Kirk. It isn't that. I simply know who I am—what I can endure—and what the rest of you cannot. When I chose to become part of the force, I had nothing to lose. Gilla's young. Her whole life is laid out before her. If I had gone mad, what would it have mattered? I would have been no worse off dying here, a raving lunatic, than dying among the Klingons, a loathsome traitor."

Kirk did not respond right away. He continued to watch Kell, becoming more and more convinced. Yes, the man was afraid. But why? And of what? A thought came to Kirk. He spoke it aloud. "What about Reni Bates? Is he part of this force too?"

Kell shook his head wearily. "Not that old fool. He's frightened to death. Of all the colonists, he was the only one who refused the Danons' offer. He was too much of a coward to reach for something higher than himself."

Gilla leaned forward in her chair, elbows balancing on her knees. "You talk of this thing as if it was a kind of test of strength. Is that what you really believe, Father?"

"In a way, I do." He was pacing again, his movements frantic and jerky. "It has to do with the will to succeed, the will to grasp power, the will to risk all that one is and has been in order to become something greater. Are you familiar with the writings of the German philosopher Friedrich Nietzsche?"

Gilla nodded silently. Kirk said, "When I was a young man—a very young man—I read Nietzsche."

"Well, read him again. Read what Nietzsche says about the will to power, about man and superman. It's what I've found here, Kirk. It's the next step in the evolution of the species."

"Nietzsche," Kirk said, "went mad."

Kell glared angrily, then laughed softly. "So he did. But I haven't." He moved toward Gilla, put out a hand, and helped draw her to her feet. For a moment, she stood away from him but then leaned forward and rested her head against his chest. Kell put his arms around her back. "Gilla, Gilla. I've missed you so much."

Kirk saw the stiffness in her spine. He could only guess at the conflicting emotions that must be raging inside her.

She stepped away from her father and made a smile. "I'm glad I've found you," she said.

"And now that you have, now that you understand what I've become, you must realize why it's necessary for you to leave Heartland."

Gilla shook her head. "No, Father. I realize why it's necessary that you should."

Kell turned his attention to Kirk, seeking help. "You tell her, Captain. You're no fool. Explain to her why what I've said is right."

"I don't think you are right."

"Then you are a fool."

"Perhaps," said Kirk. "I didn't come here to argue the point. I don't know how much of what you've said is true or false or how much you've simply held back and not told me at all. I do know this much: you're a human being, a citizen of the Federation, and you're living on a quarantined world. I can't leave this planet until you agree to come with me."

"Then you'll never leave. Not sane you won't."

"We'll see." Kirk reached past Kell and took Gilla by the hand. Together, they left the hut. Outside, the village was silent and empty. In the central clearing, the men from the *Enterprise* stood waiting. Kirk looked around. Doyle was gone.

17

Kirk brought his people together in his own hut and sketched in for them the more pertinent details of what he had learned from Kell. He had already spoken privately with Spock and McCoy and called Scotty in the *Enterprise*, ensuring that the three of them were fully aware of everything he himself knew.

"In my opinion," he said, concluding his remarks, "the only way we can be sure of leaving Heartland with Kell in our possession is to force him to come with us. If necessary, I intend to make an effort in that direction tomorrow at dawn. While Kell is only one man and there are six of us, it's impossible to estimate the amount of resistance we can expect from the Danons or from this mysterious force, whatever it is and however real. In other words, if we do move, the operation may turn out to be very easy or extremely difficult. At this time, there's just no way of knowing which. Now, are there any comments, suggestions, or words of advice?"

Crewman Mosley raised a hesitant hand. Kirk nodded in his direction. "One thing I've been thinking about, sir," Mosley said, "is Doyle's phaser. When he was returned to us, you'll remember that he didn't have any clothes on. The Danons must have his weapon. Do you think they might use it against us?"

Kirk shook his head. "I don't think this is going to be a simple matter of firepower. Whatever threat the Danons offer is a lot more subtle than that. Anything else?"

"Yes, Captain." It was Lieutenant Sulu. "I'd like to ask you about this mental force creature you described. Exactly what are its powers? How limited are they? Can it read our minds, for example?"

"All I know about this supposed entity is what Kell told me. His description was extremely vague—deliberately so, I believe—and therefore mine is too. As far as the range of its powers is concerned, I honestly do not know."

"Then it may be listening in on us right now," Crewman Schang said, glancing over his shoulder at the blank wall behind, "and we'd never even know it."

"Cowardice isn't going to get us anywhere," Mosley said gruffly.

"It's not cowardice," Schang said hotly. "I just don't think we have to be thickheaded."

Spock intervened before the situation deteriorated further. "I would regard the possibility you raised as an extremely unlikely one, Crewman Schang, although it is certainly worth considering. As a purely spiritual form of life, the mental force would not possess sensory capabilities of its own. The Danons—and Kell too—would serve as its eyes and ears. Without them, it would be deaf and blind."

"Which underscores," said Kirk, "the necessity of keeping our intentions secret. There will be no poker games like last night. If any of the Danons approach you with offers of immortality or anything else, inform me or Mr. Spock at once."

"If it happens to me, I'll tell them to go straight to hell," Schang said. He looked at Mosley as he spoke, an expression of grim determination on his face.

"Fine," said Kirk, resisting the impulse to smile. "Now is there anything else?"

Schang raised his hand. "Just one thing, sir: this man Kell. He's not crazy like Doyle and the others you told us about. Is that right?"

"Largely, yes, but I don't think Kell is totally stable either. We're going to have to deal with him as carefully as possible." He glanced at Gilla, but she made no move to dispute his analysis. "Is that all, then?"

This time no one spoke.

"All right," said Kirk. "I want to emphasize that once it's dark we're going to have to be especially cautious. I've decided to bring everyone into this hut for tonight. Two of us will stand watch for two-hour periods. I want one person inside the hut and the other outside." The reason for this was obvious— to prevent a repetition of Schang's nap the previous night—but Kirk saw nothing to be gained by emphasizing the point. Although he hadn't said so in so many words, Schang seemed properly ashamed of what he had done. And what was past was past. "Our living conditions may prove a bit crowded, but I suspect we'll manage to endure."

"Is there some particular reason why we're waiting, sir?" Lieutenant Sulu asked. "It would seem to me that we might as well take Kell now and not wait for morning."

"There are two valid reasons to proceed as I've indicated," said Kirk. His firm voice disguised the fact that he actually agreed with Sulu. His original intention had been to act at once. Gilla had dissuaded him. She insisted that she believed that Kell might still change his mind with the passage of time. Kirk thought that the real reason for her hesitancy was simply her aversion to violence. "First, I'd prefer to have Kell join us of his own free will, and I want to give him every opportunity of doing that. Second, if yesterday is any indication, the Danons are primarily nocturnal. By waiting for dawn, we strike when their resistance is weakest, when they're ready to fall asleep. Is that enough to satisfy you, Mr. Sulu?"

Sulu seemed taken aback by the sharpness of his captain's tone. "I didn't mean any criticism, sir."

"No, of course not. I'm sorry. But you can do one other thing for me, Mr. Sulu. Take Mosley and Schang into the forest and see if you can pick enough fruit to keep us full through the night. You'd better go now. I'll want you back here well before dark."

"Yes, sir."

After Sulu, Schang, and Mosley had departed, Gilla stood up and said she wanted to step out for some air. Kirk raised no objection. Alone with Spock and McCoy, he turned to them. "Well, gentlemen, what do you think? Is it worth the risk?"

"I'd say so, Jim," McCoy said. "Frankly, I don't see any alternative."

"Mr. Spock? You seem troubled."

"I have a tentative suggestion to make, Captain, something I thought best not to discuss in front of the others. Since it's the presence of the mental force that provides the only major obstacle to the success of your plan, I would be willing to undergo fusion, enter the gestalt, and attempt to counteract its strength with my Vulcan mental powers."

"And destroy yourself along with it?" Kirk shook his head firmly. "We simply don't know enough about the real nature of this entity to take that kind of risk. There's more to this force than we so far know about. With all due respect for your mental capabilities, Mr. Spock, I do not care to stand by and watch you driven mad."

Spock nodded stiffly. "As you wish, Captain."

"I'm afraid I do." He came to his feet. "Now, if you two will excuse me, I'm going out for some fresh air of my own. I'll be back before dark."

Gilla was waiting outside the hut. "Mind sharing your thoughts?" he asked her.

She shrugged. "Not in the least."

"How about a walk?"

"Here? Where can we go?"

"We'll find a place. Come on."

She laughed. "All right. Let's walk."

As Kirk and Gilla threaded through the maze of huts, heading in the general direction of the village center, the air was as still and silent as ever. Gilla said casually, "Mr. Spock wanted to join the gestalt, didn't he?"

Kirk was surprised. "How did you know?"

"I didn't listen in. I know a few things about Vulcan psychology. Something like the mental force would fascinate a creature like Spock."

"I told him not to try it."

"Were you worried he might end up like my father?"

"I was worried about his safety, yes."

"But how much is one life really worth? I'm not trying to be dramatic. I think it's an honest question. Unlike you, I put little faith in violence. I don't think we'll ever take my father away from here without his consent."

"Then let me think differently—for now."

"The Danons are the key. Don't you agree with me

about that? If they want my father to leave, he will."

"The Danons or the force?"

"Either one. It just seems to me we ought to be thinking about why he's important to them, why they don't want to let him go. He says he's revived the force. I wonder. Was it him or was it only what he represents—humanity? Could any other human being have done as well?"

"I hope you're not volunteering to take his place?"

She laughed. "I said it was just a thought."

They had reached the clearing at the center of the village. Kirk looked ahead at the stone tower. Two Danons could be seen perched at the farthest ends of the upper crossbar. A third sat in the space where the two diagonal bars intersected. Seeing Kirk and Gilla, the Danons waved their tiny hands excitedly. Kirk, after a moment's hesitation, waved back.

"Do we have to stay here?" Gilla said, her hands clenched rigidly at her sides.

"Not if you don't want to. Come on."

They turned away from the clearing and moved past the silent huts again. As they did, Gilla said, "I find it hard to keep from wondering about the meaning of this whole thing. My father spoke of merging with the force as if it was a test of strength, and I think I'm beginning to understand what he meant. We human beings are so accustomed to our separate, islandlike existences. We spend sixty, seventy, eighty years trapped inside our bodies, like clams cowering under their shells. My father went beyond that. It couldn't have been easy. I admire him for it."

"And he can live forever," Kirk said.

"Yes, and to me, as a Jain, that's important too. I believe in reincarnation. I'm sure you don't—few practical people do—but I'm convinced that the soul never dies, that it is born again and again, passing from body to body, life to life, shell to shell, until for a few—the most worthy—final release is achieved and the soul passes beyond this plane of existence to another, higher place, and the curse of continual rebirth is finally ended. My father has found that release. I envy him."

"If you do, why aren't you willing to let him stay here on Heartland?"

"Because he's not dead." She gripped his arm as she spoke, the physical contact emphasizing the intensity of her feelings. "That's why it's wrong. And he's not happy. He's achieved something magnificent but he can't appreciate it. When his body dies, maybe then it'll be different. Right now he's both alive and dead. I don't think a person can be that—and stay sane."

"Aren't you neglecting something?"

"What?"

"The nature of the mental force. Spock has had some contact with it. He told me it was full of hate. This isn't some benevolent godhead we're talking about, Gilla. It's an evil thing."

"Do you really believe that? Evil?"

"Yes, evil. I know it's a difficult word to use. We live in a time when too much is known and supposedly understood. We have psychology and psychiatry and sociology and anthropology and a dozen other sciences to tell us why people act as they do. Things like good and evil have been relegated to an ignorant, superstitious past. But sometimes I wonder. I don't like these Danons. I don't like their mental force. And either they or it—or both—has infected your father far more than he's willing to acknowledge."

Their route had carried them to the edge of the

forest. Kirk noticed a narrow path opening into the woods and gestured at Gilla to join him.

"Are you sure we ought to go in there?" she asked.

"Why not? We have time."

She followed him. They had gone only a short distance when the path suddenly swerved and the trees swallowed up any last sight of the Danon village. Kirk felt relieved. A cool breeze stirred. He walked with a lighter step than any he'd known since reaching this planet.

"I'm glad we came here," Gilla said. "It's peaceful. Dark and noisy and full of life—but peaceful."

"I like it too." He heard the same things she did: singing birds, whining insects, the whisper of leaves in the wind.

He put an arm around her waist. The trail narrowed. Kirk stopped. To one side he saw a big willowlike tree with hundreds of overhanging vines like green tendrils. He knew what it would be like underneath: a private place, cool and dark and in this climate probably dry.

"Let's go over there."

She nodded.

They went through the veil of vines. On the other side, it was exactly as Kirk had anticipated: a private place of their own.

18

Kirk stood watch outside the hut. Raising his head, he peered at the eastern sky and nodded. He was certain this time that the sky was definitely getting lighter. Dawn was coming at last. Soon it would be time to move.

"Mr. Spock," he said softly, leaning close to the open doorway.

"Here, Captain."

"It's going to be morning in a few more minutes."

"Any sign of the Danons?"

"Not a peep. It's as quiet out here as a baby's nursery."

"When will you want to commence waking the others?"

"Soon. Give them a few more minutes. Before we move, I want it to be bright enough to see without using flashlights. I'll talk to Scotty once more, then we'll start. What about you, Mr. Spock? Any problems?"

"No, Captain. The watch has been quite routine."

"I hope you're not complaining."

"Not at all."

Kirk nodded. The entire night had passed uneventfully. He and Spock had stood first watch, followed by McCoy and Mosley, Sulu and Schang. This was his second tour of duty outside the hut, Spock's second inside. So far, no one had heard a sound or seen a thing. He didn't like it this way. His plan of attack had envisioned a village of Danons exhausted from their nocturnal ramblings. Where were they? Asleep? Perhaps they didn't need to rest at all. How could he be sure they wouldn't soon be stirring too, rising with the break of day?

Kirk looked at the sky again. There was a definite dividing line between the blackness and the spreading gray. As he watched, the line crawled slowly toward the zenith. Kirk reached for his belt, tugged the communicator loose, and flipped open the antenna grid.

"Mr. Scott?"

"Here, sir."

"It's starting to get light down here. I'll be rousing the others in a few minutes. Give us twenty minutes to reach Kell and five more to have him in our hands. Be prepared to beam us up any time after that."

"We're prepared now, sir. I have guards standing by in the transporter room, and I intend to go there myself once we're finished speaking."

"I'll look forward to seeing your smiling face again, Scotty."

"Will you be coming with the initial group?"

"No. That's one of the things I wanted to tell you about. I've decided that Mosley and I will stay behind. Dr. McCoy and Mr. Spock will have the responsibility of transporting Kell."

"I was rather hoping you'd come with the first group, Captain."

"What's wrong, Scotty? The burdens of command beginning to rest heavily on your shoulders?"

"Not at all, sir. I just think—"

"I know, Scotty, I know. But I am the captain." Kirk spoke with calculated lightness. "I'm supposed to go down with the ship, aren't I?"

"This isn't a ship, sir."

"No, but I'm still a captain. Wait for our signal. I won't be able to talk to you until then."

"Captain?"

"Yes, Scotty. What else?"

"I just wanted to wish you luck, sir."

"Thank you, but why worry? We've been in a lot tougher situations than this in the past."

"I know, sir, but there's just something about this planet. Even from up here on the viewscreen, it looks like a wrong place to me."

"Well, I appreciate your wishes. We'll talk again later."

"I'll be waiting, sir."

"Fine. Kirk out."

After fastening the communicator to his belt, Kirk looked at the sky one more time. It was a flat gray sheet. All but the brightest stars had faded from view. He lowered his gaze. The outlines of the nearer huts were clearly visible. He tried to listen. Nothing. First a silent night and now a silent day. Yes, it was time to move.

Dropping to his hands and knees, he entered the hut.

Mr. Spock stood on the opposite side of the doorway. A portable lantern burned between his feet. "Now, Captain?" he asked softly.

"Yes. Go ahead and start waking them."

Spock nodded silently. Turning, he moved methodically among the sleeping bodies on the floor, waking each in turn. Kirk waited until everyone was sufficiently awake and alert, then led the way through the doorway. Mosley followed at his heels, then young

Schang, McCoy, Gilla, Spock, and Sulu. Kirk had tried to convince Gilla earlier in the day to leave Heartland and wait for her father aboard the *Enterprise*. She had refused. "When I came here, I promised myself never to leave without my father. I meant it then, Jim, and I mean it now."

In the same order in which they had left the hut, the group moved in single file, their steps as soft as falling snow. When they passed the central clearing, Kirk glanced at the tower, but there was nothing —no grinning, waving Danons—to disrupt its somber presence.

When he reached a certain hut, Kirk raised the signal to halt. Glancing past his shoulder, he caught Gilla's eye. She nodded. This was Kell's hut.

"Mosley, Spock," Kirk whispered. "You'll come with me. Sulu, Schang, station yourselves beside the doorway. Bones, let me have your britebeam. I may need it inside."

McCoy removed the britebeam from his medikit and handed it to Kirk. The instrument, a miniaturized power pack the size of a thumbnail, produced a bright laser beam.

Kirk advanced toward the hut. At the doorway, he dropped to his knees and peered inside. It was dark. Turning his head, he nodded at Sulu and Schang to assume their positions. Mosley and Spock waited behind him. Ducking his head, Kirk entered the hut in a swift, sudden motion.

He came to his feet on the other side. Darkness surrounded him. He took a step forward, feeling the soft carpet underfoot. A hand touched his shoulder. Without looking, he knew it must be Spock.

Kirk edged forward, giving Mosley room to enter as well. Then he switched on the britebeam and directed it toward the ceiling.

Kell lay curled up in a corner, apparently fast

asleep. Kirk observed him carefully. His chest rose and fell; his lips fluttered. There was absolutely no expression on the man's face.

Keeping the light fixed on the ceiling, his footsteps muffled by the carpet, Kirk advanced on Kell. He moved around the table and chairs. Spock was right behind him. Mosley remained close to the doorway. Kirk was only a short distance from Kell when the man suddenly sat bolt upright. He looked at Kirk and a smile played across his face. He shook his head. "Kirk, you fool."

"I want you to come with me," Kirk said evenly.

"Where?"

"To the *Enterprise*—my ship."

Kell stiffened. In the periphery of his vision, Kirk saw Mosley draw his phaser. "You won't make it," Kell said.

"Let's keep this peaceful," Kirk said. "Gilla's outside. For her sake, let's avoid trouble."

"This is a mistake. A stupid mistake."

"Let me be the judge of that. Are you coming, Kell? Do we have to force you?"

Kell rolled off his bed of furs and stood. He was fully dressed. "All right—I'm ready."

"Then go out first. I have more men outside. There's nothing you want to take with you?" Kirk gestured toward the paintings.

"I don't expect to be gone long." Kell dropped to his knees in front of the doorway. He looked back at Kirk. "This isn't going to work. I hope you realize that. There's no way you can force me to go anywhere against my will."

"Then let me try."

Kell shrugged and crawled through the doorway. Kirk waved at Mosley to follow. When he was gone, Spock crawled through. Still holding the britebeam, Kirk bent down.

A soft voice reached him through the doorway. "Captain Kirk?" It was Sulu.

He paused. "Yes, what is it?"

"I think we have a problem, sir."

"I'm coming out."

As soon as Kirk poked his head through the gap into the morning light, he knew what Sulu meant.

The circle spread two-deep around the surrounding huts. There were at least a hundred of them, silent and motionless, the same as before.

The Danons had gathered again.

19

Kirk looked at the aliens, then at Kell. The man was smiling as if in triumph.

"Why didn't you call me earlier?" Kirk asked Sulu.

"They must have crept up on us. I didn't even know they were there until I looked up and all of a sudden there they were. I don't know how it could have happened, sir."

"Don't worry about it. Mosley, cover Kell. If he moves a muscle, stun him."

"Gladly, sir." Mosley grinned. He apparently considered Kell at least partially responsible for what had befallen his friend Doyle.

Gilla and Dr. McCoy came running over. Gilla looked at her father, started to speak to him, then suddenly stopped. Kell looked distracted. His eyes focused distantly. His jaw was slack.

McCoy said, "What are we going to do now?" No panic invaded his voice; the question was intended honestly.

"There's only one thing we can do, Bones," Kirk said. "Proceed as before. Here—take your britebeam back. I won't be needing it now." He reached for his belt. With one eye fastened on the circle of Danons, he called the *Enterprise*. "Scotty, this is Captain Kirk. We're ready. Beam up the six I told you about thirty seconds from now."

"Aye, aye, sir."

Kirk lowered the communicator but did not sever the connection. "Bones, Spock, take hold of Kell."

As the moments passed, Kirk tried not to count each individual second. The Danons never moved. Kirk looked at the other members of his own party: Gilla was anxious, Sulu determined, Schang excited, Mosley dedicated. Spock and McCoy held Kell, one to each arm. A good group, Kirk decided. Now if he could only get them out of here.

Ten seconds, he thought. It couldn't be any longer than that.

"The force is here," Spock said softly.

"You can feel it?"

Spock nodded. "I'm trying . . ."

"No!" Kirk's voice was sharp. "Stand by to beam up. I don't want—"

In a swirl of light, Spock, McCoy, Sulu, Schang, Gilla, and Kell disappeared.

Kirk let out his breath. Now if only—

He never finished the thought.

The six who had vanished reappeared.

Kirk stared at them, momentarily stunned.

Scott's anxious voice came from the communicator: "The transporter doesn't seem to be functioning, sir. We started to receive them and then nothing."

Kirk raised the communicator to his lips. "They're back here. Try again."

"Now, sir?"

"Yes."

Spock took a step toward Kirk, releasing his hold on Kell. "Captain, I think I should—"

Again, the transporter flared. Again, the six disappeared. Again, within seconds, they were back again.

Kirk noticed a smile on Kell's face. "I told you," he said softly. "I told you it couldn't be done."

Kirk ignored him. As he spoke into the communicator, he kept his voice well under control. "Do you have any idea what's wrong, Scotty?"

"None at all, sir. I've run a computer analysis with negative results. Mechanically, there appears to be nothing wrong with the system. Should I try again?"

"No. Not right away. I think the problem may lie here."

"There, sir? But I don't—"

"Nor do I, Mr. Scott. It's what I intend to find out."

"As you wish, Captain."

Kirk approached the grinning Kell. "Let him go," he ordered McCoy, who still retained his grip on the man's arm.

"Jim, don't," Gilla said, stepping between him and her father.

"I don't intend to harm him," Kirk said.

"You can't," Kell said tauntingly. "Haven't you figured that much out? You're a beaten man, Kirk. Now why don't you get out of here and leave us alone? You've met a force far stronger than you and your machines."

Kirk shook his head wearily. At the moment it was hard to disagree with Kell. He looked at Spock and realized at once that something was wrong. The Vulcan's eyes were blank and staring, his body held rigid.

"Spock," Kirk said, moving around Gilla and Kell as if they weren't there. "What have you done to yourself?"

"Call. Ship." Spock's voice came as if from far away. "I am . . . incorporated. Call Scott and tell him to beam . . . beam up."

Kirk knew what Spock had done: linked his mind with the Danon force. He raised the communicator to his lips and spoke quickly. "Scotty, I want you to try again. Beam everyone up except myself and Spock. And do it now."

"Aye, aye, sir."

The film of perspiration covering Spock's face made his skin seem to gleam in the early morning sunlight.

There was a burst of light as the transporter took hold. Six bodies began to fade from view.

Spock screamed. It was a terrible sound of unendurable agony. He grabbed at his head and fell to the ground.

The six bodies appeared as before.

Kirk rushed forward to help Spock. The Vulcan rolled slowly on his back. He raised his arms and began striking his own face with clenched fists. Blood flowed—green, copper-based Vulcan blood. Kirk felt sick to his stomach.

He could hear Kell laughing.

"Mosley, Schang, grab his arms," Kirk cried. Kneeling down, Kirk tried to hold Spock's legs, which were kicking frantically. Sulu tried to help him. McCoy hurried over, a hypodermic already in hand.

Spock's strength was enormous. It took all four men to hold him pinned to the ground. As McCoy leaned over to inject the hypodermic, Spock suddenly stiffened. Kirk could feel every muscle in the leg he held tighten simultaneously.

Spock went limp. Kirk looked at his face. The eyes were open.

Kirk stared in horrified amazement, unable to believe what he saw.

Spock was crying. Wet tears streamed down his cheeks.

Kirk stood up. "Let him go," he said.

Mosley, Schang, and Sulu came to their feet.

Spock lay on his back on the ground, his chest heaving spasmodically.

"Should I . . . ?" said McCoy, holding up the hypodermic.

Kirk nodded.

McCoy bent swiftly down. Spock did not resist as the hypo hissed softly.

McCoy stood erect. Spock's eyes were shut. His breathing was regular.

"Is he . . . ?" Kirk said. "Will he . . . ?"

McCoy shook his head and looked away. "Your guess is as good as mine, Jim."

"The fool's gone mad!" Kell cried triumphantly. "Didn't I warn you? He tried to tamper with a force greater than himself, and now he's paid the price!"

Kirk felt too defeated to answer. "Bones, we've got to get Spock back to the ship somehow."

20

James Kirk sat on the end of a fallen log at the edge of the forest and watched as Gilla Dupree advanced on him from between two nearby huts. Her figure in the flowing dress was only dimly visible in the gathering twilight, but he had no trouble identifying her. As her footsteps came near, he turned and gazed into the forest again. Her hand fell on his shoulder.

"You shouldn't be out here alone, Captain."

He looked up at her, smiling. "Well, I'm not alone now."

"Don't tell me you knew I'd come."

"Well, actually, no. I was just trying to think."

"You were moping?"

He shook his head. "No, not really. That doesn't do much good." He patted the log beside him. "This is a strange planet, and the Danons are very strange enemies, if that's what indeed they are. No, I just wanted to try to collect my thoughts. I wanted to see if I could think this thing through."

"And?"

"I'm afraid I've found out very little. There's still

too much that we just don't know. This force can be beaten. I'm sure of that much."

"Why?"

"Because nothing's invincible, except perhaps a god, and that's not what we're dealing with here."

"How about a devil?"

"No, that's different."

She sat down beside him, folding her dress around her legs. "Aren't you being religious?"

"I don't think so, no. To me, it's also the scientific point of view: everything in creation has its own established limits."

"But you haven't found any yet. Not for this force."

"Not yet, but I will."

"I do admire your tenacity, Jim."

"Is that what it is? To tell you the truth, I'm really not sure myself. I drastically underestimated our adversary this morning, and Mr. Spock had to pay the price. Now I know better. There's a way out of this, and if I don't find it, someone else will. I have the ship's computer working overtime, analyzing every available droplet of data concerning group intelligence. There's got to be an answer."

She nodded distantly, her gaze distracted. "And what about Mr. Spock? Is he going to recover?"

Spock was no longer on Heartland. Earlier in the day, Kell had appeared at the hut to announce that there would be no interference if Kirk wished to transport Spock to the *Enterprise* for better medical care. For a moment, Kirk had thought he had seen a trace of humanity in Kell's attitude, and he had accepted the offer, sending a protesting McCoy along with Spock.

"I spoke with Dr. McCoy," Kirk said in reply to Gilla's question, "and he seems to feel there's reason to hope. Spock's condition is not the same as Doyle's. There's no indication of severe brain damage. It may be more a matter of temporary shock than permanent psychosis."

"I do hope so. I like Mr. Spock. It was my idea to come to Heartland. If you hadn't met me, none of this would have happened."

"You shouldn't blame yourself."

"Why? Isn't that what you're doing? Don't you hold yourself responsible?"

"But I am. I'm the captain."

She smiled. "I thought we'd decided your name was Jim."

He smiled too. She was sharp, quick-witted. He found that very appealing. "Tell me something honestly," he said. "What do you really think of me?"

"You want to know?"

He nodded. "I do." Although, as soon as he spoke, he felt rather foolish, like a child fishing for compliments.

Gilla took him seriously. She pondered silently for what seemed a painfully long time. "I find you one of the most complex individuals I've ever known."

He was genuinely surprised. "That's not a way I usually think of myself."

"May I make a comparison? You remind me of the patterns of a kaleidoscope."

"Is that good?"

"I think so. It means you're not rigid. You're willing to change constantly. And yet—this is what I mean by complex—you're always true to yourself at the same time. I wish I could be clearer. If it were possible, I'd love to work you into a piece. That's the only way I have for getting really close to another personality."

"How do you mean work me in?"

"As a character. Oh, not the real you, of course, not the whole person—just the framework. I build around that, and as I do, I learn more and more about the genuine individual. I've composed several short pieces around the characters of imaginary Star Fleet officers, but you're the first one I've really got to know well since my father left. And you're not at all what I'd come to expect."

"What was that?"

She shut her eyes, concentrating on a mental portrait. "Someone older. And meaner. A cold, factual, unemotional, steadfast, loyal, efficient person. A harsh but honest taskmaster."

"That sounds like Captain Bligh."

She laughed. "I didn't mean to put it so strongly. Besides, it's not you. Remember, I said you were different."

"In that case, I give my permission."

"Permission?"

"For you to work me in. Use me in a piece. I'd consider it an honor to appear in your work."

Her smile went away and she seemed disturbed. "Not now," she said. "Not here."

"I meant when you got home—to Luna."

"Oh." Her smile returned but it now seemed forced. "Maybe then I will," she said.

Kirk was looking past her. Something in the forest had caught his eye, if only peripherally, and now he was trying to spot it again. He concentrated, letting his gaze shift back and forth through the dense green underbrush. Yes. There it was. He saw it again. A patch of gray among the broad leaves of a flowering plant.

Kirk stood up. He pretended to be talking to Gilla. "Perhaps it's time you and I headed—"

Then he sprang. Reaching the bush in a few quick strides, he plunged his hands inside the concealing thicket of leaves. In no time at all, he felt something soft in his grasp. Rocking on his heels, he pulled out his prize.

It was Lola—Bates's pet piker.

The animal squirmed in Kirk's arms.

He let it go.

Reni Bates stepped out from behind a tree. "Don't hurt her," he told Kirk. "We've come back to try to help you."

21

Reni Bates sat on one end of the fallen log, Lola curled at his feet like a big ball of gray fur, while Kirk loomed above him. "I mean it, Bates," he said. "I want the truth out of you—all of it this time. I don't want you holding anything back."

Bates nodded, licking his lips. "You're sure none of those devils is skulking around?"

"We're alone. You can see that. Now talk."

Bates spread his arms in a gesture of helplessness. "Where should I begin?"

"Start with the mental force—the Danon gestalt. Kell told us about that. You never even bothered to mention it. That's what drove the colonists mad and you must have known it."

"A lie, Captain," Bates said softly.

"You admit you lied?"

"Not me." A triumphant expression spread across his face. "Kell did."

"How do you know what he said? You weren't there."

Bates reached up and touched his ears. "I was listening. Outside his hut. I heard all the lies he told."

"Then why don't you tell me the rest of it? The truth?"

"I intend to. But first I need something from you. A promise. I'd like to establish a condition."

Kirk had known all along that Bates was afraid of something. Perhaps this would help explain what. "Name your condition."

"I want to leave this planet. I want to go home. When you leave, I want your promise you'll take me with you."

"That's no problem. The law applies to you as well as Kell. You shouldn't be living here either."

"And I want amnesty," Bates said, in a much softer tone than before. He lowered his head and stared at the ground.

"Amnesty for what?"

"For what I'm about to tell you. For what I did forty years ago. I want your promise."

"Before you tell me or after?"

"Before."

Kirk thought for a moment. It seemed plain that Bates did not intend to reveal a thing until he had his amnesty. "All right," Kirk said. "You have my guarantee. I'll do everything I can to help you. I can't grant a blanket pardon. My powers are limited. What I can do, I will do."

Bates nodded slowly. His eyes remained focused on the ground. "I guess I can't ask for anything more. All right." He looked up suddenly. "Where do you want me to begin?"

"Start with the colony," Kirk said. "Start with your own role."

"That's the hardest part. But I'll do it. We all came here to build a new world. There were farmers, herders, ranchers, craftsmen. We were pioneers, the backbone of any civilized society. You've seen Heartland. It's a paradise. Why slave in the dirt to produce a few measly crops when every tree in the forest is heavy all year long with fruit ripe for the picking?"

"You do it," Gilla said, speaking for the first time since Bates had been found in the forest, "because eventually that fruit may be gone. Then what will your children eat?"

Bates frowned. "That's easy to say. When you have to do the work, it's harder. But don't get me wrong. It wasn't pure laziness. The first few months, we all worked hard, but the soil was poor. When our crops were due for planting, it rained. When they were due for harvesting, a windstorm blew up. The herd animals died mysteriously. Maybe we could have persevered, survived, endured. I don't know. I know we quit trying."

"It must have been a very harsh existence," Gilla said, with sympathy.

Bates nodded. He was speaking directly to Gilla now. Kirk decided to let him continue that way. "And Heartland made doing nothing a very tempting proposition. There were the Danons to watch, for example. None of them worked. I was the first to show an interest in them. My land was closest to the village. Oh, we'd always known they were there, but our charter required us not to interfere in their lives and we had enough work of our own to keep us all busy. Then my crops gave out. My goats and cattle and chickens died. I started spending days in the village, talking with some of the Danons. Dazi was one of them. He and I became friends. It was boredom mostly on my part, but the Danons seemed like a fascinating breed to a youngster like me who'd never left the Earth before in his life. Dazi was the one who told me about the tower. After that, everything changed."

"Tower?" said Kirk. "The one in the center of the village?"

Bates never shifted his gaze from Gilla. "That's the one. It's what Kell lied to you about. There's no Danon mental force. There's only the tower and the thing that lives inside it."

"We looked in there," Kirk said. "It was empty."

This time Bates turned his head. His eyes were distant, haunted. "The part you can see, yes. There's another door in the floor. Don't feel bad because you didn't spot it. You weren't meant to. The thing I'm telling you about is like any other devil. It dwells under the ground."

"How did you learn about this?"

"As I said, Dazi told me. The Danons were more responsive back then, more willing and able to communicate. They were younger. This is their last generation, you know. There hasn't been a child born in the village for more than a hundred years. What Dazi didn't tell me then, I discovered later through observation and deduction. The story actually begins thousands of years ago. The Danons once occupied half the Galaxy. They even visited Earth."

"That's where our legend of the devil originated," Gilla said.

Bates looked at her again and shook his head. "I don't think so. At least not for the reasons you might expect. The Danons weren't evil. Not then and maybe not even now either. They were young, energetic, expansive, and aggressive. To a caveman, anything strange coming down out of the sky is going to seem threatening."

"How does this relate to what's happening now?" Kirk said. He was becoming impatient. The darkness was nearly complete. All he could see of Bates were the highlights of his haggard face, the tiny gleaming eyes. Gilla on the other end of the log was even more indistinct. Kirk wanted to get back to the hut and his men.

"Sorry," Bates said. "I do have a tendency to ramble. Let me tell you about the Torgas, then. They were another alien race. The Danons met them near the center of the Galaxy. The Torgas weren't humanoids. Shaped like slugs, from the descriptions I've heard, slugs with tentacles. The Torgas were a young, energetic, expansive, aggressive species. When they met the Danons, war broke out. It lasted for several thousand years."

"Where are the Torgas now?" Gilla asked.

"Who knows?" Bates said. "Maybe they're completely extinct. Maybe, like the Danons, they're cowering on a single obscure planet somewhere in a neglected corner of the Galaxy. The Torgas seem to have been just slightly more savage than the Danons. They started to win the war, driving the Danons back planet by planet. Eventually, the conflict reached here, the Danon homeworld. The Danons knew they either had to make a final stand or else relinquish their right to survive as a species. By then, there were only a few hundred of them left. That's when they decided to build the tower and the thing that lives under it."

"And what is this thing?" Gilla said.

"Your Mr. Spock called it a mental force. I prefer to think of it as the Great Machine. It's a computer, but that's hardly an adequate term. The Great Machine bears the same relationship to the computer in your ship as a god does to an ordinary human being. The Danons injected the totality of their collected knowledge into the machine. Then they injected themselves. They became part of it."

"Then my father didn't really fail to tell the truth," Gilla said.

"No. He just neglected to tell you everything."

"But what was the purpose of this machine?"

"Defense," Bates said. "The Danons programmed

it for only a single purpose: to defend themselves and their planet against outside attack."

"And it succeeded?"

He nodded. "It did. The Torgas never conquered Heartland. Eventually, in fact, they must have withdrawn. By then, it was too late for the Danons to recover. And the Great Machine had taken control."

"Is it alive?" Gilla said. "You speak as if it were."

"As much alive as you or I or Kirk or Lola. The Danons came to worship the machine as a god. They even made sacrifices to it. When a child was born, it too became part of the machine."

"Until there were no more children," said Kirk, who was beginning to feel that he understood.

"Exactly," said Bates. He turned on the log, facing Kirk directly. "When your ship first arrived here, Captain, did you scan the planet with your sensors?"

"Of course."

"And what did you discover? Not about the surface. We know what that's like. About the interior of the planet—the core."

"We never scanned that," Kirk said. "There seemed to be no need."

"Too bad. I can't help wondering. More than likely, you would have found nothing, but, still, it's an interesting point of conjecture. You see, I have a theory. I believe that Heartland no longer possesses a planetary core in the strict sense of the term. I believe that Heartland and the Great Machine are one and the same."

The vast scope of such a concept—a computer the size of a planet—briefly overwhelmed Kirk. He struggled to retain his sense of perspective. "What are the exact powers this machine possesses?"

"A good question," Bates said, "but one that's difficult for me to answer. In my years here, those powers have barely been tested. I can only tell you this: the Great Machine controls the lives of everyone on this planet from birth until death and beyond."

"You make it sound like a benevolent entity," Gilla said. The darkness was complete now, her voice a disembodied presence. "Like a god."

"It depends on what you mean by benevolence," Bates said. "An intelligent creature needs a reason to live. It has to be able to envision a better future life for itself and its children. The machine took that away from the Danons. In time, I believe it killed them. I call that genocide."

"And the colonists?" Kirk said. "You still haven't explained about that."

"The machine took them." His words came slowly. "I helped."

"How?" said Kirk. "And why?"

"Dazi brought me to the tower one night. Before that, he'd told me about the machine only in veiled terms. I'd asked to see more. I thought it might help us with our crops. I remember we went through the floor and down and down and down. I remember tunnels of white plastic, hundreds of them, like a madman's maze. We came to a huge room with a high ceiling. There was a big chair with long wires growing out of it like hairs. Dazi wanted me to sit there. I wouldn't do it. I was afraid. Then he told me about the machine. About the war with the Torgas—everything. He told me, when a Danon died, because it was part of the machine, it never really died. He told me I could do the same thing. He told me I could live forever."

"And did you try it?" Gilla said.

"I would have. There was something intoxicating about the whole scene. I could never have resisted. But the machine didn't want me—not then. First, it wanted me to go out among the other colonists and tell them what I had discovered and ask them to come too. I did that. They laughed at me. But they were curious. Eventually, they came to the village. The Danons took them down. When they emerged, they were mad. Every last one of them."

"But not you?"

"No. I never tried it. I never sat in the chair. I ran. I sent a distress signal and hid in the bush. The ship came and took the others away. I've been hiding ever since. Now you know why I need amnesty. If not for me, the others would have been all right."

"You didn't force them," Gilla said.

"No."

"So why was it your fault? And not everyone goes insane. My father didn't."

"No. He must be a very strong man."

"He is," Gilla said. "And he didn't care. Maybe that's what made the difference. He didn't care if he lived or died, if he was sane or insane."

"And now the machine wants you," Bates said. "It won't let you leave—ever. I think Kell tried to help you at first. I was listening when he told you to go and I knew he was right. He helped that other man leave too. But now it's too late. The machine knows about you. It'll never let you go. It needs you too much."

"But why?" said Kirk. "Aren't the Danons enough? Why should it want us?"

"Because the Danons are dying. What can be lonelier than a god no one worships?"

Somehow Bates's final sentence was the most chilling Kirk had heard tonight. "So what do you recommend we do?"

"Destroy it."

"How?"

"Your ship is armed."

"The machine was built to defend against attack. What makes you think our phasers can harm it?"

"Aren't you even going to try?" Bates's voice was desperate. It was plain that he had no idea how to counteract the strength of the Great Machine.

Kirk stood up. "Come to my hut. I want you to tell my crew what you've told Gilla and me. Maybe among all of us—and the ship's computer—we can work out a solution and find a way off this planet."

"Sure, Captain, sure," said Bates, his voice suddenly weary. It was clear that he had expected more from Kirk and now feared that the pain of confession had been to no avail. "And maybe the sun will go nova and end all our troubles."

But he went with Kirk and Gilla into the village. Lola tagged at their heels. They skirted the central clearing and its tower and headed for the hut. At the door, Gilla suddenly hung back. She caught Kirk's arm.

"Jim, I want to talk to my father."

He was puzzled. "Why? You can't expect him to help us."

"No, it's not that. I just want to talk to him. I'll be right back."

"I don't think—"

But she was gone. Kirk tried to catch sight of her, but in the dim starlight she might as well have vanished.

Frowning, he turned to Bates. "Come on. Let's get this started."

They went into the hut.

22

When Kirk entered the hut, he found Sulu, Mosley, and Schang seated on the floor in a circle around the portable lantern. The three men looked very tired and rather anxious. When Reni Bates and Lola crawled through the doorway behind Kirk, the men also looked puzzled.

"Mr. Bates has a few things to talk about," Kirk said. "I want you to listen to what he says and tell me if it sparks any ideas."

"What happened to Gilla, sir?" Sulu asked.

"She wanted to talk to her father."

"Then she just missed him. He was here twenty minutes ago."

"Did he say what he wanted?"

"He said he wanted to make a deal. He said he thought he knew a way to get us off Heartland."

"What way?"

Sulu smiled slowly. "That he didn't say."

Reni Bates snorted. "It's a trap, Captain. Whatever you do, don't listen to him. When he speaks, it's with the voice of the Great Machine."

"What's the Great Machine?" Sulu said.

"It's what Mr. Bates has come here to tell you about," Kirk said. "Now listen to him."

While Bates repeated his story in a somewhat less disorganized fashion, Kirk went to a corner of the hut and sat down heavily on a pile of furs. He leaned his head and shoulder against the wall and rubbed his eyes. He was tired. It took all the strength he possessed just to keep his eyes from falling shut as Bates droned on.

Like Bates, he was inclined to disregard the importance of Kell's visit. Later, it might well prove necessary to strike a bargain on the Machine's terms, but Kirk wasn't quite ready to do that yet. Even if the situation did seem hopeless—a handful of men against what amounted to an entire planet—there still might be a solution. The minutes ticked by as Bates continued to talk. In spite of his exhaustion, Kirk grew more impatient—and worried. Where was Gilla? Why had she so abruptly decided to talk to her father? And how could he be sure she had even told the truth? What if the visit to her father was merely a subterfuge? What if she had actually gone to talk to someone—or something—else? He recalled certain remarks she had made earlier. His anxiety deepened.

Finally, unable to bear his worry any longer, Kirk came to his feet. "I'm going out and find Gilla," he announced.

"Do you want one of us to come along?" Sulu asked.

Kirk shook his head. "No, I'll be fine."

"You're going to Kell's hut?"

"Yes. If I'm not back in an hour, call the ship. Inform Mr. Scott to assume full command pending Mr. Spock's return to regular duty."

"Are you expecting trouble, sir?"

Kirk forced a smile. "I find that it's always wisest

to expect trouble, Mr. Sulu. That way, when one stumbles across it, there's no feeling of surprise."

"Well, I still don't like it, sir."

"Don't worry so much. If you're not careful, you'll start getting wrinkles in your forehead."

Dropping to his knees, Kirk crawled through the doorway. Once outside, he switched on McCoy's brite-beam—he had borrowed it back from him before his departure in the event of just such an expedition as this—and trained it on the landscape ahead. Then he began walking toward Kell's hut. The village felt different—changed. Before, whenever he had passed the Danon huts, as deserted as they appeared from the outside, he had never doubted that each was occupied. But not now. The huts were empty—he was sure of it—the Danons gone. Without thinking, he increased his pace until he was nearly running.

It was odd how Bates's story had totally altered his feelings concerning the Danons. No longer did he regard them as devilishly sinister creations. No. If anything, he felt sorry for them. The Danons were a once proud but now tragically dying race. How long would it take, he wondered, until humanity found itself facing a similar predicament, reduced from the splendid heights it now occupied to the depths of virtual savagery and a few forlorn mud-and-grass huts? Nothing endured forever. Space taught a person that. Even the lifetime of the universe itself was a finite thing. A moment would inexorably arrive when gravity would perform its duty and all that presently existed would collapse to near nothingness. The human race could hardly expect a better end. And when that time came, when the remnants of humanity sat huddled among the ruins of Earth, who would there be to witness this final act? Another people, Kirk guessed, a species even now struggling to survive in the cold caves of a remote planet. For some reason, he discovered a certain amount of solace in this thought. Death was mere extinction, but a lonely death was a pointless one. Did the Danons find something similarly reassuring in the presence of men among them? Was that why they smiled and waved? Were they glad to have company as they died?

Kirk reached Kell's hut. Even before he dropped to his knees and crawled inside and turned the brite-beam on the interior, he knew what he would find: nothing.

Kell wasn't home. There was no sign of Gilla Dupree.

For a long moment, Kirk stood on the carpet in the center of the hut, turning the light in his hand, revealing first one painting, then the other, then a chair, then the table.

He made up his mind. He knew where Gilla had to be. An angry moan escaped his lips.

Then he slid through the doorway, came to his feet, and ran. He had never run harder in his life. His heart slapped against his chest.

As soon as he reached the clearing in the center of the village, he stopped. Something was wrong with the tower. The doorway at the base of the structure was open wide but this time, unlike before, a stream of yellow light poured through the gap.

Kirk ran toward the doorway.

A loud voice shouted his name.

Kirk stopped and swung the britebeam toward the sound. Kell stood in the dust beside the tower. He looked incredibly old. His shoulders slumped. He lifted his head and stared dimly at Kirk. His eyes were as cold as dying suns. "Kirk," he said, his voice choked. "Kirk, it's left me."

Kirk sprinted across the clearing. He dropped the britebeam, grabbed Kell by the front of his tunic, and shook him violently. "Where is Gilla? What have you done to her?"

"Gilla?" Only the barest hint of recognition showed in his voice. "I've done nothing to Gilla. It's what she's done to me."

"Where is she? Tell me, damn it. Where is she?"

"In there. With it." His head jerked toward the tower doorway. "Don't you understand what's happened, Kirk? It's left me and gone to her. I'm alone—all alone."

Kirk let him go. He understood. Kell's words could have only a single interpretation: the Great Machine had deserted him. Why? Kirk could think of only one answer to that.

He raced through the tower doorway.

"Wait!" Kell cried. "Kirk, come back! Help me! I'm frightened! I'm alone!"

Inside the room in the base of the tower, Kirk spotted the door in the stone floor. It was open, and the light which had first attracted his attention spilled through. He dropped to his knees and looked inside. An iron ladder extended down the side of a vertical shaft. The light shined brightly. Kirk could not see the bottom.

Unhesitantly, Kirk swung his legs out over the pit. Grasping the topmost iron rung, he began to descend the ladder. Because the rungs were spaced closely together for the benefit of the smaller Danons, Kirk was able to take them two and three at a time. He tried not to think about falling. The shaft was not as deep as it had seemed from above. Approximately twenty meters from the top, Kirk reached the floor. It was made of a white hard plastic substance. His boots made a hollow sound as he turned in a circle.

Two crisscrossing tunnels made of the same substance as the floor intersected at this point, offering Kirk four possible avenues to follow. He examined

the sides of the tunnels and looked at the floor, hoping
to find some clue to suggest which path he ought
to follow. There was nothing. The tunnels might have
lain undisturbed for centuries. He cupped his hands
to his mouth. "Gilla!" he shouted. "Are you there?
It's me—it's Jim!"

No response. A thick acrid odor like mechanic's
oil pervaded the air. A steady humming noise could
be heard. Kirk leaned his ear close to one wall and
listened. The sound was louder. The Great Machine,
he thought. It lives here.

He selected one of the four passageways at random
and hurried down it. He ran, his feet banging out
a steady rhythm.

The quicker he moved, the less doubt he experienced. For some reason, he was absolutely certain he
was following the correct path. For a moment, this
certainty in itself disturbed him. Who or what was
directing his movements—and why? The machine, undoubtedly. He shoved the thought aside. He wanted
to find Gilla. Did it matter how that happened as
long as it did?

The tunnel ran through a bizarre, confusing series
of turns, loops, and swirls. It branched often, dividing
again and again. Kirk went sometimes left and sometimes right but always with sureness. He remembered
Bates's description of this hidden underground world:
a madman's maze. Yes, he thought, but who was
the madman? Where was he now?

Kirk called Gilla's name often but received no
reply. For a long time, the only noise that accompanied the sound of his feet was the steady humming
of the Great Machine. Then he heard something else.
Pausing, he listened. Voices? Ahead? He ran another
dozen meters and stopped again. He listened. This
time he was sure. Voices. And not human voices

either. They were high-pitched, shrill. Danons—chattering in their own language.

Kirk ran on. He reached his destination without warning. Turning a sharp corner, he found himself in a huge chamber with a high, almost invisible ceiling. The room was empty of furniture except for a single padded armchair that sat in the middle of the floor. Hundreds of thin black wires extended from the arms and back of the chair and disappeared into the farthest wall. The Danons stood on both sides of the chair. It appeared as if all of them were present—all one hundred or so. The chair itself was occupied.

Gilla Dupree sat rigidly in the seat.

Kirk stepped slowly toward her. She stood, swinging her head, staring without recognition. Her face was a pale blank mask. For a moment Kirk feared that she had been driven insane, the same as Spock, the same as Doyle, the same as all the others.

Then she spoke: "Jim, you came."

He stopped only a few feet away from her. "Gilla," he said haltingly. "Gilla, what have they done to you?"

"To me?" She laughed. Her voice was totally changed. Kirk felt a shiver crawl up his spine. "They've done nothing to me. I did it all myself."

"But why? Why have you done this? You knew what it would mean."

"Yes. I made a bargain . . . a trade. I gave it my soul and it gave me . . . freedom."

"Your father's?"

"And mine. I told him what I planned to do. After we talked to Bates, I knew I had no choice. He tried to stop me. The Danons helped. They knew, as the machine does, that I'm better than him. I'm younger, stronger, more energetic. The machine cast him out and took me to its heart. I survived. Now I know eternity."

"No," he said, shaking his head. "No, Gilla, you can't."

"I'll never die. I'll never be born again. I'm free—totally free. Do you know what that means? Do you know how that feels?"

"You don't know what you're saying."

"I know what I am."

He took another step toward her.

She held up a hand. "Don't, Kirk, don't try it. Leave me alone. Don't you understand that I like it here? Don't you understand that I want this?"

"I can't believe . . ."

"Go!"

The meaning of her words finally reached him. "You mean we can . . ."

"Yes. I arranged that too. I'm fighting it, making it let you—" She gripped her head suddenly and fell back into the chair. "Go!" she cried. "Hurry!"

Kirk shook his head. He knew she was right, but he just couldn't do it. "I won't leave Heartland without you."

"You must. If you don't, you'll never leave at all."

"Do you think I care? Don't you understand? I love you, Gilla. I don't want to live without you."

He ran toward her. It was a purely instinctive act. He didn't think, didn't consider, didn't examine the logical alternatives. He wanted Gilla, wanted to hold her in his arms, wanted to protect her from this monstrous invisible thing.

He never reached her chair.

The Danons rushed him.

It was the last thing he had expected. Maybe the machine—or Gilla—had ordered them to act. The force of their mass assault knocked him back. He tried to reach for his phaser, but their tiny hands were wrapped around him. Oddly, as he struggled, he could still see Gilla. She sat impassively in the chair. Her eyes were open and watching him.

He lost his balance and fell to the floor.

The Danons piled on top of him. Teeth tore at his skin. Fingers shredded his clothes. His arms and legs were pinned and he could no longer move. For some reason, he felt like laughing. What a way to die. Crushed underneath a hundred squirming devils. The air rushed out of his lungs. He could no longer breathe. He shut his eyes, opened them. The result was the same: blackness.

In the darkness, he heard two final sounds. One was laughter, high-pitched, howling, crazed. He knew it was Gilla. The other sound was less immediately identifiable. Only at the end, as consciousness faded, did he realize what it had to be.

A phaser. Someone was firing a phaser.

He forced his eyes open one more time. The light struck him suddenly, like a blinding wave. He realized he was breathing again. The air rushed into his lungs like a hard fist. His body ached in a thousand places. He blinked, struggling furiously to see.

A disembodied face swam before his eyes. A familiar face. Frightened. Worried. The lips moved and sound came out, but Kirk could not understand the words.

Then he recognized the face. He felt laughter building in his chest. What a sight to see as one was dying.

The face belonged to Crewman Albert Schang.

Then Kirk lost consciousness.

23

. . . and so my recommendation remains that the quarantine of the planet Heartland be not only maintained but more strictly enforced in the future. The mysterious machine intelligence that inhabits the planet will continue to present a clear and present danger to the general well-being of the Federation only as long as the Danon race survives. Since extinction appears to be only a matter of a relatively few years away, the situation does not appear to warrant an offensive response. Time is the ally of the Federation.

I am pleased further to report that Mr. Spock continues to make substantial progress toward a full recovery and is expected to resume his normal duties within a few days. Our passenger, Jacob Kell, is also much improved. As for Gilla Dupree, I have not mentioned her in my previous log entries because—

Captain James Kirk laid down the microphone and leaned back in his chair. He sat in the privacy of his personal quarters. Well? he asked himself impa-

148

tiently. What about Gilla Dupree? What exactly do you intend to say? The truth? That she's dead? That she's dead and alive at the same time? He shook his head. What could he possibly say?

There was a knock at the door. Frowning, Kirk turned. He had given strict orders not to be disturbed. In the days since the *Enterprise* had left Heartland, he had not once left his quarters, nor had he seen or talked with anyone in that time. The ship was in competent hands. Mr. Scott could easily handle the routine chore of guiding the *Enterprise* through space to Starbase 13. Kirk wanted to be alone. He had private wounds that needed isolation in order to heal properly.

The knock came again—more insistently.

Without thinking, Kirk said, "Come in." His own words surprised him even as he spoke.

Dr. Leonard McCoy came through the door. His expression, as he stared across the room at Kirk, concealed none of the worry he plainly felt. He balanced a covered plastic tray in his hands. "I've brought you some dinner," he said, letting the door slide softly shut behind him.

"I'm not hungry."

"Schang says you haven't had a full meal in days."

"I'm still not hungry."

McCoy dropped the tray on the table and slid into the chair opposite Kirk. "Jim," he said, "I don't like to see you doing this. There's no reason for you to go on torturing yourself this way."

"It'll end."

"When?"

"When we reach Starbase 13. Until then, I intend to go on as I have. Look, Bones, I failed. I'm the captain. If anyone stayed on Heartland, it should have been me. It should never have been her . . . Gilla. It's my fault that it ever happened at all."

"I don't happen to agree."

"And what the hell business is it of yours?"

"I thought I was your friend," McCoy said gently.

Kirk frowned. He shook his head. He felt tired, spent, drained of emotion. He rubbed his unshaven cheeks. "All right. I'm sorry. You are my friend. But, damn it, what else can I think? She was young, vibrant, and alive. The whole human race lost something precious when she gave herself up to that thing back there. It was a waste—a dreadful waste. That's what bothers me the most. She had so damn much to live for, and it was my responsibility."

"That's what I came to tell you, Jim. You're wrong about Gilla. She had nothing to live for."

Kirk stared. "What do you mean by that?"

"Exactly what I said. She didn't. Gilla Dupree was and is a very sick woman. Remember her dizzy spells? Gilla has a tumor, one too advanced to be treated even by laser. Gilla will be dead inside the month. If she isn't already."

"No," said Kirk, almost soundlessly. "Why . . . why didn't you tell me before?"

"Because I'd promised. The first time I examined her—at the starbase—I had a suspicion. Later, here, when she collapsed in the herbarium, I confirmed it. She told me she knew all about it. She made me swear not to tell anyone. Especially you. And her father."

"I don't . . ."

"Well, I do. Think about it, Jim. What kind of person is Gilla Dupree? Why do you think she was so desperate to find Kell? She wanted to see him once more before she died. She gave up the last few days of her life so that he could have years."

"And he doesn't know," said Kirk. There was bitterness in his voice.

"He does now. I told him. Ten minutes ago. Before I came here."

"But she never told me."

Leaning forward, McCoy laid a hand on Kirk's arm. "Gilla Dupree was too much of a woman to burden you with something like that."

"But if she had. Damn it, if only she'd told me, I would have—"

"What?" said McCoy. "What difference would it have made? You still wouldn't have let her stay on Heartland. She knew that. She did the right thing. And, if you think about it long enough and hard enough, you'll come to the same conclusion."

"I hope you're right, Bones."

"I am." He stood up slowly. "I'd better go now. Mr. Spock keeps harassing my medics, and I think it's time I wrote out a clearance returning him to active duty." He went to the door, opened it, and stood half in and half out of the room. "Eat your dinner, Jim. You don't want to starve."

The door closed behind him.

Alone again, Kirk tried to do as McCoy had suggested: think. He thought about Heartland, the Danons, and the Great Machine.

Most of all, he thought about Gilla Dupree.

In the end, as McCoy had predicted, he came to believe that Gilla had indeed done the only right thing.

And in the end, when he had reconciled himself to the correctness of her actions and the inevitability of her death, only then could he truly grieve.

He did so.

When he finished, Kirk moved his chair close to the table and ate the meal McCoy had brought for him. It was cold but delicious.

Then he called the bridge. "Mr. Scott, this is Captain Kirk. Anything to report?"

Scott couldn't quite manage to conceal either his surprise or his delight. "Not a thing, sir, I'm pleased to say. Everything here is very, very routine. Mr. Spock was here a moment ago. I understand he will be returning to duty later in the day."

"As will I, Mr. Scott. I'll be with you in a few moments."

"I'm very pleased to hear that, sir."

"And I'm very pleased with the job you've done in my . . . my absence."

"Oh, it was nothing, Captain."

"Let me be the judge of that, Scotty."

"Aye, aye, sir."

Kirk went into the bathroom that occupied a corner of his quarters and gazed at the tired, worn, red-eyed face that greeted him in the mirror there. He shaved, took a shower, and changed into a clean uniform.

Just as he was finishing, another knock sounded at the door. Unhesitantly, Kirk said, "Come in, please."

Crewman Schang opened the door and poked his head tentatively through. Seeing the empty tray on the table, he said, "Should I take that away, sir?"

"Get in here, Schang."

"Sir?"

"I said get in here. And shut the door. I want to have a talk with you."

Schang entered with a gulp. He stopped in front of Kirk, brought his heels smartly together, and saluted crisply.

Kirk returned the gesture. "You saved my life back on Heartland, you know."

Schang looked embarrassed. "Oh, it wasn't just me, sir. Mr. Sulu and Crewman Mosley were down there too. It was just luck that I happened to be the one to pull you out from under those aliens."

"My luck, yes. My good luck. It was a damned

brave thing for you to do. I intend to recommend the three of you for fleet citations."

Schang grinned. "Why, thank you, sir."

"And one other thing," said Kirk. "As much as I've valued your work as my steward, the fact is, with Doyle's disability, I now have a shortage of security guards. Unless for some reason you'd rather stay here, I'd like to offer you the chance to change jobs. Security is a lot more interesting work than this, and you'll have a better chance at advancement."

Schang could barely control his delight. "Does that mean I'm part of the crew, sir?"

"You were always part of the crew, Schang. Always."

Kirk followed Schang out of the room. While the crewman headed for the mess, Kirk rode the turbolift to the bridge. He entered to a moment of embarrassed silence. After a few seconds, Ensign Chekov cleared his throat and began telling Lieutenant Sulu a story, the point of which seemed to be why no Russian dogs ever froze during Russian winters.

Grateful to Chekov and his fertile mind, Kirk sat down in his command chair.

In front of him, the viewscreen showed the broad expanse of Galactic space. For a long peaceful interval, Kirk simply sat and stared at the screen. He realized he was grinning. It was good to be home.

ABOUT THE AUTHOR

GORDON EKLUND has produced several science fiction novels, and anthologized several short story collections. He was awarded the prestigious Nebula Award jointly with Gregory Benford for the story "If the Stars Are Gods." He lives in California with his family.

Space, the final frontier
These are the voyages of the starship *Enterprise*™ . . .

STAR TREK®

*Join the captain and crew on these exciting and
classic journeys across space and time!*

WORLD WITHOUT END by Joe Haldeman
___24714-5 $4.99/$5.99 in Canada

THE STARLESS WORLD by Gordon Eklund
___24675-5 $4.99/$5.99 in Canada

THE FATE OF THE PHOENIX
by Sondra Marshak and Myrna Culbreath
___27932-7 $4.99/$5.99 in Canada

MUDD'S ENTERPRISE by J. A. Lawrence
___56982-1 $4.99/$5.99 in Canada

PLANET OF JUDGMENT by Joe Haldeman
___24168-0 $4.99/$5.99 in Canada

DEATH'S ANGEL by Kathleen Sky
___24983-5 $4.99/$5.99 in Canada

*Be sure to look for all the Bantam STAR TREK books on sale now
wherever Bantam Books are sold, or use this page to order.*